STARGIRL

THE EXCHANGE

Should people
change for
others?

STARGIRL

by **Jerry Spinelli**

 HAMPTON-BROWN

Many thanks to Nick Uliano, Tony Coia, and Mike Oliver
for helping me tell this story,
and to my editor, Joan Slattery

Stargirl by Jerry Spinelli
Text copyright © 2000 by Jerry Spinelli
Cover illustration copyright © 2000 by Alfred A. Knopf
Published by arrangement with Random House Children's Books
a division of Random House, Inc. New York, New York, U.S.A. All rights reserved.

On-Page Coach™ (introductions, questions, on-page glossaries), The Exchange,
back cover summary © Hampton-Brown.

Hampton-Brown
P.O. Box 223220
Carmel, California 93922
800-333-3510
www.hampton-brown.com

Printed in the United States of America

ISBN-13: 978-0-7362-3141-1
ISBN-10: 0-7362-3141-2

09 10 11 12 13 14 15 10 9 8 7 6 5

To Eileen,
my Stargirl

And to Loren Eiseley,
who taught us that even as we are,
we are becoming

And to Sonny Liston

INTRODUCTION

Jerry Spinelli knew he wanted to be a writer when he was sixteen. He wrote a poem about a school football game. It was published in the newspaper.

Spinelli kept writing. He would write during his lunch break at work. His first books were for adults. After twelve years of trying, he had not published a single book. His luck changed when he wrote *Space Station Seventh Grade*. This was a book for children instead of adults. People loved it. Spinelli has gone on to win many awards as a writer for children and young adults.

Spinelli began writing notes for *Stargirl* in 1966. The setting is a high school near the Arizona desert. Spinelli said high school was a time of "scratching around for what and who I wanted to be." His characters in *Stargirl* each search for his or her own identity.

The students of Mica High seem typical. There are athletes, cheerleaders, and other groups. Stargirl is the new girl at Mica High. The students do not know how to react to her. Mica students like people to conform. They think Stargirl is

Key Concepts

identity *n.* person's unique personality and characteristics
typical *adj.* similar to others in a group

7

weird. She has a pet rat. She is too **independent**. She likes to walk alone in the desert. She does not seem to care what other people think about her. She is different from everyone at Mica High.

But Leo Borlock can't stop thinking about her. She is so different that she makes him uncomfortable. Leo has been at Mica High long enough to know the "rules." Everyone should be the same. But something about Stargirl makes him wonder: Is being like everybody else all that interesting?

Spinelli's *Stargirl* challenges readers to think about popularity, rejection, and true friendship. Whose **opinion** matters the most? Should Stargirl change to be like everyone else? Or should everyone else change to be more like Stargirl?

Spinelli has written over fifteen books for young people, and *Stargirl* is one of his most popular. It is about the real problems students have every day. It is a story about the power of groups. But mostly, it is about the excitement of being who you are.

Key Concepts

conform *v.* to change in order to be like other people

independent *adj.* doing things or making decisions alone

opinion *n.* personal feeling or judgment

PORCUPINE NECKTIE

When I was little, my uncle Pete had a necktie with a porcupine painted on it. I thought that necktie was just about the neatest thing in the world. Uncle Pete would stand patiently before me while I ran my fingers over the silky surface, half expecting to be stuck by one of the **quills**. Once, he let me wear it. I kept looking for one of my own, but I could never find one.

I was twelve when we moved from Pennsylvania to Arizona. When Uncle Pete came to say good-bye, he was wearing the tie. I thought he did so to give me one last look at it, and I was grateful. But then, **with a dramatic flourish**, he **whipped off** the tie and draped it around my neck. "It's yours," he said. **"Going-away present."**

I loved that porcupine tie so much that I decided to start a collection. Two years after we settled in Arizona, the number of ties in my collection was still one. Where do you find a porcupine necktie in Mica, Arizona—or anywhere else, for that matter?

....

quills sharp porcupine spikes
with a dramatic flourish excitedly
whipped off quickly took off
"Going-away present." "A gift because you are moving."

On my fourteenth birthday, I read about myself in the local newspaper. The family section **ran a regular feature** about kids on their birthdays, and my mother had called in some info. The last sentence read: "As a hobby, Leo Borlock collects porcupine neckties."

Several days later, coming home from school, I found a plastic bag on our front step. Inside was a gift-wrapped package tied with yellow ribbon. The tag said "Happy Birthday!" I opened the package. It was a porcupine necktie. Two porcupines were tossing darts with their quills, while a third was **picking its teeth**.

I inspected the box, the tag, the paper. Nowhere could I find the giver's name. I asked my parents. I asked my friends. I called my uncle Pete. Everyone denied knowing anything about it.

At the time I **simply considered the episode a mystery**. It did not occur to me that I was being watched. We were all being watched.

....

ran a regular feature always had a story

picking its teeth cleaning its teeth with the quills

simply considered the episode a mystery decided to quit trying to find out who gave me the gift

I

"Did you see her?"

That was the first thing Kevin said to me on the first day of school, eleventh grade. We were waiting for the bell to ring.

"See who?" I said.

"Hah!" **He craned his neck, scanning the mob.** He had witnessed something remarkable; it showed on his face. He grinned, still scanning. "You'll know."

There were hundreds of us, milling about, calling names, pointing to summer-tanned faces we hadn't seen since June. Our interest in each other was never **keener** than during the fifteen minutes before the first bell of the first day.

I punched his arm. "Who?"

The bell rang. We **poured** inside.

I heard it again in homeroom, a whispered voice behind me as we said the Pledge of Allegiance:

"You see her?"

I heard it in the hallways. I heard it in English and Geometry:

"Did you see her?"

Who could it be? A new student? A spectacular blonde from California? Or from back East, where many of us came from? Or one of those summer makeovers, someone who leaves in June looking like a little girl and returns in September as a full-bodied woman, a ten-week miracle?

....

He craned his neck, scanning the mob. He looked around the big crowd of students.

keener stronger

poured went

And then in Earth Sciences I heard a name: "Stargirl."

I turned to the senior slouching behind me. "Stargirl?" I said. "What kind of name is that?"

"That's it. Stargirl Caraway. She said it in homeroom."

"*Stargirl?*"

"Yeah."

And then I saw her. At lunch. She wore an off-white dress so long it covered her shoes. It had ruffles around the neck and cuffs and looked like it could have been her great-grandmother's wedding gown. Her hair was the color of sand. It fell to her shoulders. Something was strapped across her back, but it wasn't a book bag. At first I thought it was a miniature guitar. I found out later it was a **ukulele**.

She did not carry a lunch tray. She did carry a large canvas bag with a life-size sunflower painted on it. The lunchroom was dead silent as she walked by. She stopped at an empty table, laid down her bag, slung the instrument strap over her chair, and sat down. She pulled a sandwich from the bag and started to eat.

Half the lunchroom kept staring, half started **buzzing**.

Kevin was grinning. "Wha'd I tell you?"

I nodded.

"She's in tenth grade," he said. "I hear **she's been home-schooled till now**."

"Maybe that explains it," I said.

Her back was to us, so I couldn't see her face. No one sat with her, but at the tables next to hers kids were cramming two

---

ukulele small Hawaiian guitar

buzzing talking quietly about Stargirl

she's been home-schooled till now she never went to a public school before and learned everything at home to a seat. She didn't seem to notice. She seemed **marooned in a sea of staring, buzzing faces**.

Kevin was grinning again. "You thinking what I'm thinking?" he said.

I grinned back. I nodded. *"Hot Seat."*

Hot Seat was our in-school TV show. We had started it the year before. I was producer/director, Kevin was on-camera host. Each month he interviewed a student. So far, most of them had been honor student types, athletes, model citizens. Noteworthy in the usual ways, but not especially interesting.

Suddenly Kevin's eyes boggled. The girl was picking up her ukulele. And now she was strumming it. And now she was singing! Strumming away, bobbing her head and shoulders, singing, "I'm looking over a four-leaf clover that I overlooked before." Stone silence all around. Then came the sound of a single person clapping. I looked. It was the lunch-line cashier.

And now the girl was standing, slinging her bag over one shoulder and marching among the tables, strumming and singing and strutting and twirling. Heads swung, eyes followed her, mouths hung open. **Disbelief.** When she came by our table, I got my first good look at her face. She wasn't gorgeous, wasn't ugly. A sprinkle of freckles crossed the bridge of her nose. Mostly, she looked like a hundred other girls in school, except for two things. She wore no makeup, and her eyes were the biggest I had ever seen, **like deer's eyes caught in headlights**. She twirled as she went past, her flaring

----

marooned in a sea of staring, buzzing faces all by herself in a crowd of staring, talking students

Disbelief. No one could believe she was dancing and singing.

like deer's eyes caught in headlights with a surprised look skirt brushing my pant leg, and then she marched out of the lunchroom.

From among the tables came three slow claps. Someone whistled. Someone yelped.

Kevin and I **gawked** at each other.

Kevin held up his hands and **framed a marquee** in the air. "*Hot Seat!* **Coming Attraction**—Stargirl!"

I slapped the table. "Yes!"

We **slammed hands.**

....

gawked stared with surprise

framed a marquee pretended there was a movie title

Coming Attraction The next exciting show will be about

slammed hands hit each other's hands with excitement

BEFORE YOU MOVE ON...

1. **Author's Style** Reread page 12. How does the author make the reader want to know more?

2. **Inference** Stargirl is not like other students at Leo's school. How can you tell?

LOOK AHEAD How does Leo feel about Stargirl? Read pages 17–28 to find out.

16

2

When we got to school the next day, Hillari Kimble was holding court at the door.

"She's not real," Hillari said. She was sneering. "She's an actress. It's a scam."

Someone called out, "Who's scamming us?"

"The administration. The principal. Who else? Who cares?" Hillari wagged her head at the absurdity of the question.

A hand flashed in the air: "Why?"

"School spirit," she spat back. "They think this place was **too dead** last year. They think if they **plant some nutcase** in with the students—"

"Like they plant **narcs** in schools!" someone else shouted.

Hillari glared at the speaker, then continued,

"—some nutcase who **stirs things up**, then maybe all the little students will go to a game once in a while or join a club."

"Instead of making out in the library!" chimed another voice. And everybody laughed and the bell rang and we went in.

Hillari Kimble's theory spread throughout the school and was widely accepted.

"You think Hillari's right?" Kevin asked me. "Stargirl's a plant?"

I snickered. "Listen to yourself."

He spread his arms. "What?"

....

too dead not exciting enough

plant some nutcase put someone different

narcs spies; people who monitor what is happening

stirs things up gets everyone excited

17

"This is Mica Area High School," I reminded him. **"It's not a CIA operation."**

"Maybe not," he said, "but I hope Hillari's right."

"Why would you hope that? If she's not a real student, we can't have her on *Hot Seat*."

Kevin wagged his head and grinned. "As usual, Mr. Director, you fail to see the whole picture. We could use the show to expose her. Can't you see it?" He did the marquee thing with his hands: "*Hot Seat* Uncovers **Faculty Hoax!**"

I stared at him, "You *want* her to be a fake, don't you?"

He grinned ear to ear. "Absolutely. **Our ratings will go sky-high!**"

I had to admit, the more I saw of her, the easier it was to believe she was a plant, a joke, anything but real. On that second day she wore bright-red baggy shorts with a bib and shoulder straps—overall shorts. Her sandy hair was pulled back into twin plaited pigtails, each tied with a bright-red ribbon. A rouge smudge appled each cheek, and she had even dabbed some oversized freckles on her face. She looked like Heidi. Or Bo Peep.

At lunch she was alone again at her table. As before, when she finished eating, she took up her ukulele. But this time she didn't play. She got up and started walking among the tables. She stared at us. She stared at one face, then another and another. The kind of bold, I'm-looking-at-you stare you almost never get from people, especially strangers. She appeared to be

....

"It's not a CIA operation." "The U.S. government is not sending people to watch us."

Faculty Hoax Teachers' Trick

Our ratings will go sky-high! A lot of people will watch our show!

looking for someone, and the whole lunchroom had become very uncomfortable.

As she approached our table, I thought: *What if she's looking for me?* The thought terrified me. So I turned from her. I looked at Kevin. I watched him grin goofily up at her. He wiggled his fingers at her and whispered, "Hi, Stargirl." I didn't hear an answer. I was intensely aware of her passing behind my chair.

She stopped two tables away. She was smiling at **a pudding-bodied** senior named Alan Ferko. The lunchroom was dead silent. She started strumming the uke. And singing. It was "Happy Birthday." When she came to his name she didn't sing just his first name, but his full name:

"Happy Birthday, dear Alan Fer-kooooh"

Alan Ferko's face turned red as Bo Peep's pigtail ribbons. **There was a flurry of whistles and hoots, more for Alan Ferko's sake, I think, than hers.** As Stargirl marched out, I could see Hillari Kimble across the lunchroom rising from her seat, pointing, saying something I could not hear.

"I'll tell you one thing," Kevin said as we joined the mob in the hallways, "she better be fake."

I asked him what he meant.

"I mean if she's real, she's in big trouble. How long do you think somebody who's *really* like that is going to last around here?"

Good question.

....

a pudding-bodied an overweight

There was a flurry of whistles and hoots, more for Alan Ferko's sake, I think, than hers. People were yellling and whistling to tease Alan Ferko, not Stargirl.

Mica Area High School—MAHS—was not exactly a **hotbed of nonconformity.** There were **individual variants here and there**, of course, but within pretty narrow limits we all wore the same clothes, talked the same way, ate the same food, listened to the same music. Even our dorks and nerds **had a MAHS stamp on them.** If we happened to somehow distinguish ourselves, we quickly snapped back into place, like rubber bands.

Kevin was right. It was unthinkable that Stargirl could survive—or at least survive unchanged—among us. But it was also clear that Hillari Kimble was at least half right: this person calling herself Stargirl may or may not have been a faculty plant for school spirit, but whatever she was, she was not real.

She couldn't be.

Several times in those early weeks of September, she showed up in something outrageous. A 1920s flapper dress. An Indian buckskin. A kimono. One day she wore a denim miniskirt with green stockings, and crawling up one leg was a parade of enamel ladybug and butterfly pins. "Normal" for her were long, floor-brushing pioneer dresses and skirts.

Every few days in the lunchroom she serenaded someone new with "Happy Birthday." I was glad my birthday was in the summer.

In the hallways, she said hello to perfect strangers. The seniors couldn't believe it. They had never seen a tenth-grader so bold.

....

hotbed of nonconformity place where people who were different could feel welcome

individual variants here and there a few people who were a little different

had a MAHS stamp on them were like everyone else

In class she was always flapping her hand in the air, asking questions, though the question often had nothing to do with the subject. One day she asked a question about **trolls**—in U.S. History class.

She made up a song about isosceles triangles. She sang it to her Plane Geometry class. It was called "Three Sides Have I, But Only Two Are Equal."

She joined the cross-country team. Our home meets were held on the Mica Country Club golf course. Red flags showed the runners the way to go. In her first meet, out in the middle of the course, she turned left when everyone else turned right. They waited for her at the finish line. She never showed up. She was dismissed from the team.

One day a girl screamed in the hallway. She had seen a tiny brown face pop up from Stargirl's sunflower canvas bag. It was her pet rat. It rode to school in the bag every day.

One morning we had a rare rainfall. It came during her gym class. The teacher told everyone to come in. On the way to the next class they looked out the windows. Stargirl was still outside. In the rain. Dancing.

We wanted to **define her, to wrap her up** as we did each other, but we could not seem to get past "weird" and "strange" and "goofy." Her ways **knocked us off balance**. A single word seemed to hover in the cloudless sky over the school:

HUH?

....

trolls fictional creatures; monsters

define her, to wrap her up decide who she was, to understand her

knocked us off balance confused us

Everything she did seemed to **echo Hillari Kimble**: She's not real . . . She's not real . . .

And each night in bed I thought of her as the moon came through my window. I could have lowered my shade to make it darker and easier to sleep, but I never did. In that moonlit hour, I **acquired a sense of the otherness of things.** I liked the feeling the moonlight gave me, as if it wasn't the opposite of day, but its underside, its private side, when the fabulous purred on my snow-white sheet like some dark cat come in from the desert.

It was during one of these nightmoon times that **it came to me** that Hillari Kimble was wrong. Stargirl *was* real.

....

echo Hillari Kimble agree with what Hillari Kimble said

acquired a sense of the otherness of things was able to see things in a different way

it came to me I realized

3

We fought daily, Kevin and I.

My main job as producer was to **recruit people for** the Hot Seat. After I signed someone up, Kevin began researching the person, getting his questions ready.

Every day he asked me, "Did you sign her up?"

Every day I answered no.

He got frustrated.

"What do you mean, no? Don't you *want* to sign her up?"

I told him I wasn't sure.

His eyes bugged out. "Not sure? How can you not be sure? We high-fived in the lunchroom weeks ago. We were thinking Stargirl mini-series, even. This is a *Hot Seat* **from heaven**."

I shrugged. "That was then. Now I'm not sure."

He looked at me like I had three ears. "What's there to be not sure about?"

I shrugged.

"Well then," he said, "*I'll* sign her up." He walked away.

"You'll have to find another director, then," I said.

He stopped. I could **almost see the steam rising from his shoulders**. He turned, pointed. "Leo, you can be a real jerk sometimes." He walked off.

It was uncomfortable. Kevin Quinlan and I usually agreed on everything. We had been best friends since arriving in Arizona the same week four years before. We both thought

----

recruit people for get people to be on

***Hot Seat* from heaven** perfect idea for our show

almost see the steam rising from his shoulders see how angry he was the prickly pear cactus looked like Ping-Pong paddles with whiskers, and that saguaros looked like dinosaur mittens. We both loved strawberry-banana smoothies. We both wanted to go into television. Kevin often said he wanted to be a sleazy talk show host, and he wasn't kidding. I wanted to be a sports announcer or news anchor. We conceived *Hot Seat* together and convinced the faculty to let us do it. It was an instant hit. It quickly became the most popular thing in school.

So why was I balking?

I didn't know. I had some vague feelings, but the only one I could identify was a warning: Leave her alone.

In time "Hillari's Hypothesis" (so called by Kevin) about Stargirl's origins gave way to other theories.

She was trying to get herself discovered for the movies.

She was **sniffing fumes**.

She was homeschooling gone **amok**.

She was an alien.

The rat she brought to school was only the **tip of the iceberg**. She had hundreds of them at home, some as big as cats.

She lived in a ghost town in the desert.

She lived in a bus.

Her parents were circus acrobats.

Her parents were witches.

Her parents were **brain-dead vegetables** in a hospital in Yuma.

We watched her sit down in class and pull from her canvas

---

sniffing fumes taking drugs

amok wrong

tip of the iceberg beginning of something bigger

brain-dead vegetables in comas

bag a blue and yellow ruffled curtain that she draped over three sides of her desk. We saw her set out a three-inch clear glass vase and drop into it a white and yellow daisy. She did and undid this in every class she attended, six times a day. Only on Monday mornings was the daisy fresh. By last period the petals were drooping. By Wednesday the petals began to fall, the stem to sag. By Friday the flower hung down over the rim of the waterless vase, its dead stump of a head shedding yellow dust in the pencil groove.

We joined her as she sang "Happy Birthday" to us in the lunchroom. We heard her greet us in the hallways and classrooms, and we wondered how she knew our names and our birthdays.

Her caught-in-headlights eyes **gave her a look of perpetual astonishment**, so that we found ourselves turning and looking back over our shoulders, wondering what we were missing.

She laughed when there was no joke. She danced when there was no music.

She had no friends, yet she was the friendliest person in school.

In her answers in class, she often spoke of sea horses and stars, but she did not know what a football was.

She said there was no television in her house.

She was **elusive**. She was today. She was tomorrow. She was the faintest scent of a cactus flower, the flitting shadow of an elf owl. We did not know what to **make of her**. In our minds

....

gave her a look of perpetual astonishment made her look surprised all the time

elusive hard to understand or describe

make of her think about her

we tried to pin her to a corkboard like a butterfly, but the pin merely went through and away she flew.

Kevin wasn't the only one. Other kids pestered me: "Put her on the Hot Seat!"

I lied. I said she was only a tenth-grader and you had to be at least a junior to be on *Hot Seat.*

Meanwhile, I **kept my distance**. I observed her as if she were a bird in an aviary. One day I turned a corner and there she was, coming right at me, the long skirt softly rustling, looking straight at me, surrounding me with those eyes. I turned and trotted off the other way. Seating myself in my next class, I felt warm, shaken. I wondered if my foolishness showed. Was I myself becoming goofy? The feeling I had had when I saw her around the corner had been something like panic.

Then one day after school I followed her. I kept at a safe distance. Since she was known not to take a bus, I expected the walk to be short. It wasn't. We trekked all over Mica, past hundreds of grassless stone-and-cactus front yards, through the Tudorized shopping center, skirting the electronics business park around which the city had been invented a mere fifteen years before.

At one point she pulled a piece of paper from her bag. She consulted it. She seemed to be reading house numbers as she walked along. Abruptly she turned up a driveway, went to the front door, and left something in the mailbox.

I waited for her to move off. I looked around—no one on

....

**we tried to pin her to a corkboard like a butterfly, but the
pin merely went through and away she flew** we tried to
figure her out and study her, but we could not

kept my distance stayed away

the street. I went to the mailbox, pulled out a homemade card, opened it. Each tall letter was a different painted color. The card said: CONGRATULATIONS! It was unsigned.

I resumed following her. Cars pulled into driveways. It was dinnertime. My parents would be wondering.

She took the rat from the bag and put it on her shoulder. Riding there, the rat faced backward, its tiny triangular face peeping out of her sand-colored hair. I could not see its beady black eyes, but I guessed it was looking at me. I fancied it was telling her what it saw. I fell farther back.

Shadows crossed the streets.

We passed the car wash and the bike shop. We passed the country club golf course, the biggest spread of green grass until the next golf course in the next town. We passed the "Welcome to Mica" sign. We were walking westward. There was us and the highway and the desert and the sun blazing above the Maricopa Mountains. I wished I had my sunglasses.

After a while she **veered** from the highway. I **hesitated**, then followed. She was walking directly into the setting sun, now a great orange perched atop the mountain crests. For a minute the mountains were the same dusky lavender as her sand-skimming skirt. With every step the silence grew, as did my sense that she knew—had known all along—that she was being followed. Or more, that she was leading me. She never looked back.

She strummed her ukulele. She sang. I could no longer see the rat. I imagined it was **dozing in the curtain of** her hair.

....

Shadows crossed the streets. Time passed.
veered moved away
hesitated paused
dozing in the curtain of sleeping in

I imagined it was singing along. The sun **lay down** behind the mountains.

Where was she going?

In the gathering dusk, the saguaros flung shadows of giants across the pebbled earth. The air was cool on my face. The desert smelled of apples. I heard something—a coyote? I thought of rattlesnakes and scorpions.

I stopped. I watched her walk on. **I stifled an impulse to call after her,** to warn her . . . of what?

I turned and walked, then ran, back to the highway.

....

lay down set

I stifled an impulse to call after her I did not let myself call her name

BEFORE YOU MOVE ON...

1. **Evidence and Conclusions** Reread pages 19 and 23. Leo does not like Stargirl at first. How do you know?

2. **Inference** Why does Leo follow Stargirl into the desert?

LOOK AHEAD Read to page 45 to find out what crazy thing Stargirl does next.

4

At Mica Area High School, Hillari Kimble was famous for three things: her mouth, The Hoax, and Wayne Parr.

Her mouth spoke for itself, most often to complain.

The episode that became known as Hillari's Hoax took place in her sophomore year, when she tried out for cheerleading. Her face and hair and figure were right enough, and she surely had the mouth—she made the squad easily. And then she stunned everyone by turning it down. She said she just wanted to prove that she could do it. She said she **had no intention of yammering and bouncing** in front of empty bleachers (which was usually the case). And anyway, she hated sports.

As for Wayne Parr, he was her boyfriend. Mouthwise, he was her opposite: he seldom opened his. He didn't have to. All he had to do was appear. That was his job: appear. By both girls' and boys' standards, Wayne Parr was gorgeous.

But he was more—and less—than that.

In terms of achievement, Wayne Parr seemed to be nobody. He played on no sports team, joined no organization, won no awards, earned no A's. He was elected to nothing, honored for nothing—and yet, though I did not realize this until years later, he was **grand marshal of our daily parade**.

We did not wake up in the morning and ask ourselves, "What will Wayne Parr wear today?" or "How will Wayne Parr

---

Her mouth spoke for itself She was always talking

had no intention of yammering and bouncing was not going to yell, jump, or cheer

grand marshal of our daily parade our leader

act today?" At least, not consciously. But on some level below awareness, that is exactly what we did. Wayne Parr did not go to football and basketball games, and **by and large**, neither did we. Wayne Parr did not ask questions in class or get worked up over teachers or pep rallies, and neither did we. Wayne Parr did not much care. Neither did we.

Did Parr create us, or was he simply a reflection of us? I didn't know. I knew only that if you **peeled off one by one all the layers of the student body**, you would have found at the core not the spirit of the school, but Wayne Parr. That's why, in our sophomore year, I had recruited Parr for the Hot Seat. Kevin was surprised.

"Why him?" Kevin said. "What's he ever done?"

What could I say? That Parr was a worthy subject precisely *because* he did nothing, *because* he was so monumentally good at doing nothing? I had only a vague insight, not the words. I just shrugged.

The highlight of that *Hot Seat* came when Kevin asked Parr who was his hero, his role model. It was one of Kevin's standard questions.

Parr answered, "*GQ.*"

In the control room, I did a double take. Was the sound working right?

"*GQ?*" Kevin repeated dumbly. "*Gentleman's Quarterly?* The magazine?"

Parr did not look at Kevin. He looked straight at the camera. He nodded smugly. He went on to say he wanted to

....

by and large most of the time

peeled off one by one all the layers of the student body looked at all of the different groups of students become a male model, his ultimate ambition was to be on the cover of *GQ*. And right there he posed for the camera—**he had that disdainful model look down pat**—and suddenly I could see it: the jaw square as the corner of a cover, the **chiseled** cheeks, the perfect teeth and hair.

That, as I say, took place toward the end of our sophomore year. I thought then that Wayne Parr would always **reign as** our grand marshal. How could I have known that he would soon be challenged by a freckle-nosed homeschooler?

....

he had that disdainful model look down pat just like a real model

chiseled attractive, masculine

reign as be

5

The call came from Kevin on a Friday night. He was at the football game. "Quick! Hurry! **Drop** whatever you're doing! Now!"

Kevin was one of the few who went to games. The school kept threatening to drop football because of low attendance. They said ticket receipts were barely enough to pay for electricity to light the field.

But Kevin was screaming on the phone. I jumped in the family **pickup** and raced to the stadium.

I **bolted** from the truck. Kevin was at the gate, windmilling his arm: "Hurry!" I threw the two dollar admission at the ticket window and we raced for the field. "See better up here," he said, yanking me into the stands. It was **halftime**. The band was on the field, all fourteen of them. Among the students it was known as "The World's Smallest Standing Band." There weren't enough of them to form recognizable letters or shapes—except for a capital "I" —so they didn't march much at halftimes of games. They mostly stood. In two rows of seven each, plus the student conductor. No majorettes. No color guard. No flag and rifle girls.

Except this night. This night Stargirl Caraway was on the field with them. As they played, rooted in their places, she pranced around the grass in her bare feet and long lemon-yellow dress. She roamed from goalpost to goalpost. She

....

Drop Stop
pickup truck
bolted ran quickly
halftime the break in the middle of the game

swirled like a dust devil. She marched stiffly like a wooden soldier. She tootled an imaginary flute. She **pogoed** into the air and knocked her bare heels together. The cheerleaders gaped from the sidelines. A few people in the stands whistled. The rest—they barely outnumbered the band—sat there **with *What is this?* on their faces**.

The band stopped playing and marched off the field. Stargirl stayed. She was twirling down the forty-yard line when the players returned. They did a minute of warm-up exercises. She joined in: jumping jacks, belly whomps. The teams lined up for the second half kickoff. The ball perched on the kicking tee. She was still on the field. The referee blew his whistle, pointed to her. He flapped his hand for her to go away. Instead, she dashed for the ball. She plucked it off the tee and danced with it, spinning and hugging it and hoisting it into the air. The players looked at their coaches. The coaches looked at the officials. The officials blew their whistles and began **converging on** her. The sole policeman on duty headed for the field. She punted the ball over the visiting team's bench and ran from the field and out of the stadium.

Everyone cheered: the spectators, the cheerleaders, the band, the players, the officials, the parents running the hot dog stand, the policeman, me. We whistled and stomped our feet on the aluminum bleachers. The cheerleaders stared up in delighted surprise. For the first time, they were hearing something come back from the stands. They did cartwheels and backflips and even a three-tier pyramid. Old-timers—or as old as timers got

....

swirled like a dust devil spun like dust in a strong wind
pogoed jumped
with *What is this?* on their faces looking very confused
converging on moving toward

in a city as young as Mica—said they had never heard **such a racket**.

For the next home game more than a thousand people showed up. Everyone but Wayne Parr and Hillari Kimble. There was a line at the ticket window. The refreshment stand ran out of hot dogs. A second policeman was called in. The cheerleaders were in their glory. They screamed up at the bleachers: "GIMME AN E!" The bleachers screamed back: "EEEE!" (We were the Electrons, in honor of the town's electronics heritage.)

The cheerleaders ran through all their routines before the first quarter was over. The band was loud and peppy. The football team even scored a touchdown. In the stands heads kept swinging to the edges of the field, to the entrance, to the streetlamp-lighted darkness behind the stadium. **The sense of expectation grew** as the first half came to a close. The band marched smartly onto the field. Even they were looking around.

The musicians did their program. They even formed a small, lopsided circle. They seemed to linger on the field, drawing out their notes, waiting. Finally, reluctantly, they marched to the sideline. The players returned. They kept glancing around as they did their warm-ups. When the referee raised his arm and blew his whistle for the second half to begin, **a sense of disappointment fell over the stadium**. The cheerleaders' shoulders sagged.

She wasn't coming.

....

such a racket so much noise

The sense of expectation grew Everyone was hopeful

a sense of disappointment fell over the stadium everyone seemed sad and disappointed

On the following Monday, we **got a shock** in the lunchroom. Bleached blonde and beautiful Mallory Stillwell, captain of the cheerleaders, was sitting with Stargirl. She sat with her, ate with her, talked with her, walked out with her. By sixth period the whole school knew: Stargirl had been invited to become a cheerleader and had said yes.

People in Phoenix must have heard us buzzing. Would she wear the usual skirt and sweater like everyone else? Would she do the usual cheers? Did all the cheerleaders want this, or was it just the captain's idea? Were they jealous?

Cheerleading practice drew a crowd. At least a hundred of us stood by the parking lot that day, watching her learn the cheers, watching her jump around in her long pioneer dress.

She spent two weeks practicing. Halfway through the second week she wore her uniform: green-trimmed white V-neck cotton sweater, short green and white pleated skirt. She looked just like the rest of them.

Still, to us she was not truly a cheerleader, but Stargirl dressed like one. She continued to strum her ukulele and sing "Happy Birthday" to people. She still wore long skirts on non-game days and **made a home of her school desks**. When Halloween arrived, everyone in her homeroom found a candy pumpkin on his or her desk. No one had to ask who did it. By then most of us had decided that we liked having her around. We found ourselves looking forward to coming to school, to seeing what **bizarre antic she'd be up to**. She gave us something to talk about. She was entertaining.

....

got a shock were surprised

made a home of her school desks decorated her desks as if they were in her home

bizarre antic she'd be up to strange thing she would do

At the same time, we held back. Because she was different. *Different.* We had no one to compare her to, no one to measure her against. **She was unknown territory.** Unsafe. We were afraid to get too close.

Also, I think we were all waiting to see the outcome of an event that **loomed larger and larger with every passing day.** The next birthday coming up was Hillari Kimble's.

....

She was unknown territory. No one knew anyone or anything like her.

loomed larger and larger with every passing day was coming soon

6

Hillari herself **set the stage** the day before. In the middle of lunch, she got up from her table and walked over to Stargirl. For half a minute she just stood behind Stargirl's chair. Silence everywhere except for tinklings in the kitchen. Only Stargirl was still chewing. Hillari moved around to the side.

"I'm Hillari Kimble," she said.

Stargirl looked up. She smiled. She said, "I know."

"My birthday is tomorrow."

"I know."

Hillari paused. Her eyes narrowed. She jabbed her finger in Stargirl's face. "Don't try singing to me, I'm warning you."

Only those at nearby tables heard Stargirl's faint reply: "I won't sing to you."

Hillari **gave a satisfied smirk** and walked off.

From the moment we arrived at school the next day, the **atmosphere bristled like cactus paddles**. When the buzzer sounded for first lunch, we leaped for the doors. We swarmed into the food lines. We raced through our choices and hurried to our seats. Never had we moved so fast so quietly. At most, we whispered. We sat, we ate. We were afraid to crunch our potato chips, afraid we might miss something.

Hillari was first to enter. She marched in, leading her girlfriends **like an invading general**. In the food line, she

....

set the stage took control of the situation
gave a satisfied smirk smiled meanly
atmosphere bristled like cactus paddles mood was tense
like an invading general with power and purpose

smacked items onto her tray. She glared at the cashier. While her friends scanned the crowd for Stargirl, Hillari stared ferociously at her sandwich.

Wayne Parr came in and sat several tables away, as if even he was afraid of her on this day.

Stargirl finally came in. She went straight to the food line, **blithely smiling** as usual. Both she and Hillari seemed unaware of each other.

Stargirl ate. Hillari ate. We watched. Only the clock moved.

A kitchen staffer stuck her head out over the conveyor belt and called: "Trays!"

A voice barked back: "Shut up!"

Stargirl finished her lunch. As usual, she stuffed her wrappings into her paper bag, carried the bag to the paper-only can by the tray return window, and dropped it in. She returned to her seat. She picked up the ukulele. We stopped breathing. Hillari stared at her sandwich.

Stargirl began strumming and humming. She stood. She strolled between the tables, humming, strumming. Three hundred **pairs of eyes followed her.** She came to Hillari Kimble's table—and kept on walking, right up to the table where Kevin and I sat with the *Hot Seat* crew. She stopped and she sang "Happy Birthday." It was Hillari's name at the end of the song, but **true to her word of** the day before, she did not sing it *to* Hillari—she sang it to me. She stood at my shoulder and looked down at me, smiling and singing, and I didn't know whether to look down at my hands or up at her face, so I did

....

blithely smiling smiling very happily
pairs of eyes followed her people watched her
true to her word of like she had said

some of each. **My face was burning.**

When she finished, the students burst from their silence with wild applause. Hillari Kimble stomped from the lunchroom. Kevin looked up at Stargirl and pointed at me and said what everyone must have been thinking: "Why him?"

Stargirl tilted her head, as if studying me. She grinned mischievously. She tugged on my earlobe and said, "He's cute." And walked off.

I was feeling **nine ways at once, and they all ended up at the touch of her hand on my ear**—until Kevin reached over and yanked the same earlobe. "This keeps getting more interesting," he said. "I think it's time to go see Archie."

....

My face was burning. I was very embarrassed.

nine ways at once, and they all ended up at the touch of her hand on my ear many different emotions throughout my body, especially where she touched my ear

7

A. H. (Archibald Hapwood) Brubaker lived in a house of bones. Jawbones, hipbones, femurs. There were bones in every room, every closet, on the back porch. Some people have stone cats on their roofs; on his roof Archie Brubaker had a skeleton of Monroe, his deceased Siamese. Take a seat in his bathroom and you found yourself facing the faintly smirking skull of Doris, **a prehistoric creodont**. Open the kitchen cabinet where the peanut butter was kept and you were face to fossil face with an extinct fox.

Archie was not morbid; he was a **paleontologist**. The bones were from digs he had done throughout the American West. Many were rightly his, found in his spare time. Others he collected for museums but slipped into his own pocket or knapsack instead. "Better to sit in my refrigerator than disappear in a drawer in some museum basement," he would say.

When he wasn't digging up old bones, Archie Brubaker was teaching at universities in the East. He retired at the age of sixty-five. When he was sixty-six, his wife, Ada Mae, died. At sixty-seven he moved himself and his bones west, "to join the other fossils."

He chose his home for two reasons: (1) **its proximity** to the high school (he wanted to be near kids; he had none of his own) and (2) "Señor Saguaro." Señor Saguaro was a cactus, a thirty-foot-tall giant that towered over the toolshed in the backyard.

....

a prehistoric creodont an animal that lived millions of years ago

paleontologist scientist who studied the bones of animals

its proximity how close it was

It had two arms high on the trunk. One stuck straight out; the other made a right turn upward, as if waving "adiós!" The waving arm was green from the elbow up; all else was brown, dead. Much of the thick, leathery skin along the trunk had come loose and crumpled in a heap about the massive foot: **Señor Saguaro had lost his pants.** Only his ribs, thumb-thick vertical timbers, held him up. Elf owls nested in his chest.

The old professor often talked to Señor Saguaro—and to us. He was not certified to teach in Arizona, but that did not stop him. Every Saturday morning his house became a school. Fourth-graders, twelfth-graders—all were welcome. No tests, no grades, no attendance record. Just the best school most of us had ever gone to. He **covered** everything from toothpaste to tapeworms and somehow made it all fit together. He called us the Loyal Order of the Stone Bone. He gave us homemade necklaces. The pendant was a small fossil bone strung on rawhide. Years before, he had told his first class, "Call me Archie." He never had to say it again.

After dinner that day, Kevin and I walked over to Archie's. Though the official class **convened** on Saturday morning, kids were welcome anytime. "My school," he said, "is everywhere and always in session."

We found him, as usual, on the back porch, rocking and reading. The porch, bathed in the red-gold light of sunset, faced the Maricopas. Archie's white hair seemed to give off a light of its own.

The moment he saw us, he put down his book. "Students!

....

Señor Saguaro had lost his pants. The outer skin of the giant cactus had fallen down like a man's pants.

covered taught us about

convened met

Welcome!"

"Archie," we said, then turned to greet the great cactus, as visitors were expected to do: "Señor Saguaro." We saluted.

We sat on rockers; the porch was full of them. "So, men," he said, "**business or pleasure?**"

"**Bafflement**," I said. "There's a new girl in school."

He laughed. "Stargirl."

Kevin's eyes popped. "You know her?"

"Know her?" he said. He picked up his pipe and loaded it with cherrysweet tobacco. He always did this when settling in for a long lecture or conversation. "Good question." He lit the pipe. "Let's say she's been on the porch here quite a few times." White smoke puffed like Apache signals from the corner of his mouth. "I was wondering when you'd start asking questions." He chuckled to himself. "Bafflement . . . good word. She *is* different, isn't she?"

Kevin and I burst into laughter and nods. At that moment I realized how much I had been craving Archie's confirmation.

Kevin exclaimed, "Like another species!"

Archie cocked his head, as if he had just caught the sound of a rare bird. The pipe stem anchored a wry grin. A sweet scent filled the air about our rocking chairs. He stared at Kevin. "**On the contrary**, she is one of us. Most decidedly. She is us more than we are us. She is, I think, who we really are. Or were."

Archie talked that way sometimes, in riddles. We didn't always know what he was saying, but our ears didn't much care. We just wanted to hear more. As the sun dipped below the

....

business or pleasure? are you here to talk about something serious or something fun?

Bafflement Confusion

On the contrary Actually

mountains, it fired a final dart at Archie's flashing eyebrows.

"She's homeschooled, you know. Her mother brought her to me. I guess she wanted **a break from playing teacher**. One day a week. Four, five—yes, five years now."

Kevin pointed. "You created her!"

Archie smiled, puffed. "No, that was done long before me."

"Some people are saying she's some kind of alien sent down here from **Alpha Centauri** or something," said Kevin. He chuckled, but not too convincingly. He half believed it.

Archie's pipe had gone out. He relit it. "She's anything but. She's an earthling if there ever was one."

"So it's not just an act?" said Kevin.

"An act? No. If anybody is acting, it's us. She's as real as"—he looked around; he picked up the tiny, wedgelike skull of Barney, a 60-million-year-old Paleocene rodent, and held it up—"as real as Barney."

I felt **a little jolt of pride** at having reached this conclusion myself.

"But the name," said Kevin, leaning forward. "Is it real?"

"The name?" Archie shrugged. "Every name is real. That's the nature of names. When she first showed up, she called herself Pocket Mouse. Then Mudpie. Then—what?— Hullygully, I believe. Now . . . "

"Stargirl." The word came out whispery; my throat was dry.

Archie looked at me. "Whatever strikes her fancy. Maybe that's how names ought to be, heh? Why be stuck with just one your whole life?"

....

a break from playing teacher someone else to teach Stargirl sometimes

Alpha Centauri a distant star; somewhere far away

a little jolt of pride proud

"What about her parents?" said Kevin.

"What about them?"

"What do they think?"

Archie shrugged. "I guess they agree."

"What do they do?" Kevin said.

"Breathe. Eat. Clip their toenails."

Kevin laughed. "You know what I mean. Where do they work?"

"Mrs. Caraway, until a few months ago, was Stargirl's teacher. I understand she also makes costumes for movies."

Kevin poked me. "The crazy clothes!"

"Her father, Charles, works—" he smiled at us "—**where else?**"

"MicaTronics," we said **in chorus**.

I said it with wonder, for I had imagined something more **exotic**.

Kevin said, "So where is she from?"

A natural question in a city as young as Mica. Nearly everybody had been born somewhere else.

Archie's eyebrows went up. "Good question." He took a long pull on the pipe. "Some would say Minnesota, but in her case . . . " He let out the smoke, his face disappearing in a gray cloud. A sweet haze veiled the sunset: cherries roasting in the Maricopas. He whispered, "**Rara avis**."

"Archie," said Kevin, "you're not making a lot of sense."

Archie laughed, "Do I ever?"

....

where else? where everyone else works.

in chorus together

exotic unusual

Rara avis Rare bird (in Latin)

Kevin jumped up. "I want to put her on *Hot Seat*. **Dorko Borlock here** doesn't want to."

Archie studied me through the smoke. I thought I saw approval, but when he spoke, he merely said, "**Work it out**, men."

We talked until dark. We said "adiós" to Señor Saguaro. On our way out, Archie said, more to me than to Kevin, I thought: "You'll know her more by your questions than by her answers. Keep looking at her long enough. One day you might see someone you know."

....

Dorko Borlock here Leo Borlock is being stupid and
Work it out Decide what to do together

BEFORE YOU MOVE ON...

1. **Cause and Effect** Stargirl performs at the football game. What happens because of this?

2. **Character's Motive** Reread page 45. Archie does not tell the boys how to solve their problem. Why not?

LOOK AHEAD Read to page 58 to find out why the students start to like Stargirl.

8

The change began around Thanksgiving. By December first, Stargirl Caraway had become the most popular person in school.

How did it happen?

Was it the cheerleading?

The last football game of the season was her first as a cheerleader. **The grandstand was packed**: students, parents, alumni. Never had so many people come to a football game to see a cheerleader.

She did all the regular cheers and routines. And more. In fact, she never stopped cheering. While the other girls were taking breaks, she went on jumping and yelling. She **roamed**. Areas that had always been ignored—the far ends of the grandstand, the spectators behind the goalposts, the snack bar parents—found themselves with their own arm-pumping cheerleader.

She ran straight across the fifty-yard line and joined the other team's cheerleaders. We laughed as they stood there with their mouths open. She cheered in front of the players' bench and was **shooed away** by a coach. At halftime she played her ukulele with the band.

In the second half she got acrobatic. She did cartwheels and backflips. At one point the game was stopped and three

....

The grandstand was packed Everyone was there
roamed walked everywhere
shooed away dismissed; told to leave

zebra-shirted officials ran toward one end zone. She had **shinnied** up a goalpost, tightrope-walked out to the middle of the crossbar, and was now standing there with her arms raised in a touchdown sign. She was commanded down, **to a standing ovation and flashing cameras**.

As we filed out afterward, no one mentioned how boring the game itself had been. No one cared that the Electrons had lost again. In his column next day, the sports editor of the *Mica Times* referred to her as "the best athlete on the field." We couldn't wait for basketball season.

Was it a Hillari Kimble backlash?

Several days after the birthday song, I heard a shout down the hallway: "Don't!" I ran. A crowd was gathered at the top of a stairwell. They were all staring at something. I pushed my way through. Hillari Kimble was standing at the upper landing, grinning. She was holding Cinnamon the rat, dangling by its tail over the railing, nothing but space between it and the first floor. Stargirl was on the steps below, looking up.

The scene froze. The bell for the next class rang. Nobody moved. Stargirl said nothing, merely looked. The eight toes of Cinnamon's front paws splayed apart. Its tiny unblinking eyes were bulging, black as cloves. Again a voice rang out: "Don't, Hillari!" Suddenly Hillari dropped it. Someone screamed, but the rat fell only to the floor at Hillari's feet. She sent Stargirl a final sneer and left.

....

shinnied climbed

to a standing ovation and flashing cameras while everyone stood and clapped and took her picture

Was it Dori Dilson?

Dori Dilson was a brown-haired ninth-grader who wrote poems in a looseleaf notebook half as big as herself and whose name nobody knew until the day she sat down at Stargirl's table for lunch. Next day the table was full. No longer did Stargirl eat lunch—or walk the hallways or do anything else at school—alone.

Was it us?

Did we change? Why didn't Hillari Kimble drop the rat to its death? Did she see **something** in our eyes?

Whatever the reason, by the time we returned from Thanksgiving break, it was clear that the change had occurred. Suddenly Stargirl was not dangerous, and we rushed to **embrace her.** Calls of "Stargirl!" flew down the hallways. We couldn't say her name often enough. It tickled us to mention her name to strangers and watch the expressions on their faces.

Girls liked her. Boys liked her. And—most remarkable—the attention came from all kinds of kids: **shy mice and princesses, jocks and eggheads.**

We honored her by imitation. A chorus of ukuleles strummed in the lunchroom. Flowers appeared on classroom desks. One day it rained and a dozen girls ran outside to dance. The pet shop at the Mica Mall ran out of rats.

The best chance for us to express our admiration came in the first week of December. We were gathered in the

....

something judgment

embrace her make her a part of our group

shy mice and princesses, jocks and eggheads shy kids and popular girls, athletes and smart kids auditorium for the annual oratorical contest. Sponsored by the Arizona League of Women Voters, the event was open to any high school student who cared to show his or her stuff as a public speaker. The microphone was yours for seven minutes. Talk about anything you like. The winner would move on to the district competition.

Usually only four or five students entered the contest at MAHS. That year there were thirteen, including Stargirl. You didn't have to be a judge to see that she was far and away the best. She gave an **animated** speech—a performance, really—titled "Elf Owl, Call Me by My First Name." Her gray-brown homesteader's dress was the color of her subject. I couldn't see her freckles from the audience, but I imagined them dancing on her nose as she flicked her head this way and that. When she finished, we stomped on the floor and whistled and shouted for more.

While the judges **went through the charade of conferring**, a film was shown. It was a brief documentary about the previous year's state finals. It featured the winner, a boy from Yuma. The most riveting moments of the film came not during the contest, but **during its aftermath**. When the boy arrived back at Yuma High, the whole school mobbed him in the parking lot: banners, cheerleaders, band music, confetti, streamers. Pumping his arms in the air, the returning hero rode their shoulders into school.

The film ended, the lights went on, and the judges proclaimed Stargirl the winner. She would now go on to the

....

animated exciting

went through the charade of conferring pretended that they had to decide who was the best

during its aftermath after the contest

district competition in Red Rock, they said. The **state finals** would be held in Phoenix in April. Again and again we whooped and whistled.

Such was the acclamation we gave her in those last weeks of the year. **But we also gave something to ourselves.**

....

state finals final competition for the state

Such was the acclamation That was the kind of praise

But we also gave something to ourselves. But we were also very proud of ourselves.

9

In the Sonoran Desert there are ponds. You could be standing in the middle of one and not know it, because the ponds are usually dry. Nor would you know that inches below your feet, frogs are sleeping, their heartbeats down to once or twice per minute. They lie dormant and waiting, these mud frogs, for without water their lives are incomplete, they are not fully themselves. For many months they sleep like this within the earth. And then the rain comes. And a hundred pairs of eyes pop out of the mud, and at night a hundred voices call across the moonlit water.

It was wonderful to see, wonderful to be in the middle of: **we mud frogs awakening all around. We were awash in tiny attentions.** Small gestures, words, empathies thought to be extinct came to life. For years the strangers among us had passed sullenly in the hallways; now we looked, we nodded, we smiled. If someone got an A, others celebrated, too. If someone sprained an ankle, others felt the pain. We discovered the color of each other's eyes.

It was **a rebellion** she led, a rebellion *for* rather than against. For ourselves. For the dormant mud frogs we had been for so long.

Kids whose voices had never been heard before spoke up in class. "Letters to the Editor" filled a whole page of the school newspaper's December edition. More than a hundred students

....

we mud frogs awakening all around we acted like frogs that were waking up

We were awash in tiny attentions. We noticed the small things.

a rebellion like a war

tried out for the Spring Revue. One kid started a camera club. Another wore Hush Puppies instead of sneakers. A plain, timid girl painted her toenails kelly green. A boy showed up with purple hair.

None of this was publicly acknowledged. There were no PA announcements, no TV coverage, no headlines in the *Mica Times*:

MAHS STUDENTS ASTIR
INDIVIDUALITY ERUPTS

But it was there; it was happening. I was used to peering through the lens, to framing the picture, and I could see it. I could feel it in myself. I felt lighter, unshackled, as if something I had been carrying had fallen away. But I didn't know what to do about it. **There was no direction to my liberation.** I had no urge to color my hair or trash my sneakers. So I just enjoyed the feeling and watched the once amorphous student body separate itself into hundreds of individuals. **The pronoun "we" itself seemed to crack and drift apart in pieces.**

Ironically, as we discovered and distinguished ourselves, a new collective came into being—a vitality, a presence, a spirit that had not been there before. It echoed from the rafters in the gym: "GO, ELECTRONS!" It sparkled in the water fountains. At the holiday assembly, the words of the alma mater had wings.

"It's a miracle!" I gushed to Archie one day.

He stood on the edge of his back porch. He did not turn.

....

There was no direction to my liberation. I did not know what to do now that I was free.

The pronoun "we" itself seemed to crack and drift apart in pieces. Everyone felt like an individual, not just part of a group.

He pulled the pipe slowly from between his lips. He spoke as if to Señor Saguaro or to the blazing mountains beyond.

"Best hope it's not," he said. "The trouble with miracles is, they don't last long."

And the trouble with bad times is, you can't sleep through them.

It was a golden age, those few weeks in December and January. How could I know that when the end came, I would be **in the middle of it?**

....

It was a golden age It was a new, wonderful time

in the middle of it part of the problem; the reason for the end

10

All my resistance to putting Stargirl on *Hot Seat* vanished. "Okay," I said to Kevin, "let's do it. Schedule her." He started off. I grabbed his arm. "Wait—ask her first."

He laughed. "Right. Like she's gonna say no."

No one had ever said no to the Hot Seat. Any reluctance to answering personal or embarrassing questions always **yielded to the lure of** appearing on TV. If anyone could resist that lure, I figured it would be Stargirl. That day after school, Kevin came at me thumbs-up and grinning: "It's a go! She said yes!"

First I was surprised. This didn't fit my impression of her. I didn't know that this was an early glimpse of something I was soon to see much more of: behind the dazzling talents and differentness, she was far more normal than I had realized.

Then I was elated. We yipped. We high-fived. We saw visions of our most popular show ever.

This was mid-January. We set a date of February thirteenth, the day before Valentine's. We wanted a full month for buildup. With my resistance now gone, I **jumped in with both feet**. **We planned a promo campaign.** We got art students to do posters. We jotted down questions for Kevin to ask in case the jury ran out—fat chance of that happening. We didn't have to post the usual jury notice: dozens of kids volunteered.

And then things changed again.

---

yielded to the lure of was less important than
jumped in with both feet started working right away
We planned a promo campaign. We came up with ways to let everyone know about the show.

In the courtyard of our school stood a five-foot sheet of plywood in the shape of a roadrunner. It was a bulletin board, strictly for student use, always taped and tacked with messages and announcements. One day we found the following computer printout taped to the plywood roadrunner:

"I pledge allegiance to United Turtles of America and to the fruit bats of Borneo, one planet in the Milky Way, incredible, with justice and black bean burritos for all."

Handwritten across the bottom were the words: "This is how she says the Pledge of Allegiance."

No one had to tell us who "she" was. Apparently, she was overheard in homeroom as we said the Pledge each morning.

As far as I knew, we were not **a particularly patriotic bunch**. I didn't hear people saying they were offended. Some thought it was funny. Some giggled and nodded knowingly, as if to say, **There she goes again**. On the following mornings, more than one kid was heard reciting the new "pledge."

Within days a new story **wildfired through the student body**. A senior girl, Anna Grisdale, lost her grandfather after a long illness. The funeral took place on a Saturday morning. For a while everything seemed routine: the crowd of people at the church, the line of cars with their headlights on, the smaller group clustered around the grave for the final farewell. After the brief graveside service, the funeral director handed everyone a long-stemmed flower. Upon leaving, each mourner laid his or her flower over the casket. This was when Anna

....

a particularly patriotic bunch passionately loyal to our country

There she goes again Stargirl is being funny again

wildfired through the student body was being told by everyone at school

Grisdale first noticed Stargirl.

Through her own tears Anna could see that Stargirl was crying also. She wondered if Stargirl had been at the church as well. Even more, she wondered why Stargirl was there at all. Could she have been friends with her grandfather without Anna's knowing it? Anna's mother asked her who the unfamiliar girl was.

Afterward, the mourners were invited to Anna's house for lunch. About thirty came. There was a **buffet of cold cuts** and salads and cookies. Stargirl was there, chatting with members of the family but not eating or drinking anything.

Suddenly Anna heard her mother's voice. It was no louder than the others, but it was different: "What are you doing here?"

Sudden stillness. Everyone staring.

They were in front of the picture window. Anna had never seen her mother so angry. Mrs. Grisdale had been very close to her father. They had built an addition to their house so he could live with them.

She glared down at Stargirl. "Answer me."

Stargirl gave no reply. "You didn't even know him, did you?"

Still Stargirl said nothing.

"*Did* you?"

And then Anna's mother was **flinging open** the front door and pointing, as if **banishing her** to the desert. "Leave my house."

Stargirl left.

----

buffet of cold cuts table covered with deli meat

flinging open quickly opening

banishing her sending her forever

Danny Pike was nine years old. He loved to ride the bicycle he had gotten for his birthday. One day after school he lost control and plowed into a mailbox. He broke his leg, but that wasn't the worst of it. **A blood clot developed.** He was airlifted to Children's Hospital in Phoenix, where he was operated on. For a while **it was touch and go**, but within a week he was on his way back home.

All this was reported in the *Mica Times*. As was the celebration when Danny arrived at his home on Piñon Lane. The five-column photo in the *Times* showed Danny on his father's shoulders, surrounded by a mob of neighbors. In the foreground was a new bike, and a big sign that read:

WELCOME HOME, DANNY

It wasn't until days later that the front-page photo appeared on the plywood roadrunner. We gathered around to see something we hadn't noticed before. An arrow from a thick red felt-tip marker pointed at one of the tiny faces crowded into the frame. It was the face of a girl, beaming as if Danny Pike were her little brother back from the dead. It was Stargirl.

And then there was the bike.

The various members of the Pike family—parents, grandparents, **et al.**—each thought someone else had bought Danny the new bicycle. Several days went by before they discovered to their great surprise that none of them had.

....

A blood clot developed. His blood could not flow correctly in his leg.

it was touch and go his health was bad

et al. and others

So where did the bike come from? High-schoolers who heard the story and saw the picture had a pretty good idea. Apparently the Pikes did not. The bike became the focus of a family **squabble**. Mr. Pike was mad because nobody he asked would admit to buying the bike—and probably because he hadn't done it himself. Mrs. Pike was mad because no way, not for at least one year, would she allow Danny back on wheels.

One night the new, still-unridden bike wound up at the Pikes' front curb with the trash cans. By the time the trash collector came the next day, it was gone. Danny got a BB gun instead.

The Pledge of Allegiance, the Grisdale funeral, the Danny Pike affair—these things were noted, but they **had no immediate impact on** Stargirl's popularity at school. **Not so with** cheerleading and the boys' basketball season.

....

squabble argument, fight

had no immediate impact on did not instantly change

Not so with It was not the same for

BEFORE YOU MOVE ON...

1. **Paraphrase** What does Leo mean when he says on page 48: "We honored her by imitation"?

2. **Conclusions** Who is putting the notes about Stargirl on the roadrunner? Why?

LOOK AHEAD Read to page 72. What stops Stargirl from cheering?

II

During the **first quarter** of each home game, Stargirl went over to the visitors' section and gave them a cheer. She began with an exaggerated ball-bouncing motion:

> *Dribble, Dribble!*
> *Sis Boom Bibble!*
> *We don't bite!*
> *We don't nibble!*
> *We just say—*
> (sweeping wave)
> *"Howwww-dee, friends!"*
> (two thumbs pointing to her chest)
> *"We're the Electrons!"*
> (points to them)
> *"Who—are—YYYYYYOU?"*
> *(turns head to side, cups ear)*

A couple of visiting cheerleaders, maybe a fan or two would call back: "Wildcats!" or "Cougars!" or whatever, but most of them just gaped at her as if to say, Who is *this*? Some of her fellow cheerleaders were amused, some were **mortified**.

At that point the only crime Stargirl could have been accused of would be **corniness**. But she didn't stop there. She cheered whenever the ball went in the basket, regardless of

....

first quarter first part
mortified very embarrassed
corniness silliness

which team shot it. It was the strangest sight: the other team scores, the MAHS crowd **sits glumly on their hands** while Stargirl, alone, pops up cheering.

At first the other cheerleaders tried to **suppress** her; it was like trying to calm down a puppy. When they gave her the pleated skirt, they made a cheerleader they never imagined. She did not limit herself to basketball games. She cheered anyone, anything, anytime. She cheered the big things—honors, election winners—but she gave most of her attention to little things.

You never knew when it would happen. Maybe you were a little ninth-grade nobody named Eddie. As you're walking down the hall you see a candy wrapper on the floor. You pick it up and throw it in the nearest trash can—and suddenly there she is in front of you, pumping her arms, her honey hair and freckles flying, swallowing you whole with those enormous eyes, belting out a cheer she's making up **on the spot**, something about Eddie, Eddie and the trash can teaming up to wipe out litter. A mob is gathering, clapping hands in rhythm, more eyes on you than all the previous days of your life combined. You feel foolish, exposed, stupid. You want to follow the candy wrapper into the trash can. It's the most painful thing that's ever happened to you. Your brain keeps squirting out a single thought: *I'm going to die . . . I'm going to die . . .*

And so, when she finally finishes and her freckles settle back onto the bridge of her nose, why don't you? Why don't you just die?

....

sits glumly on their hands looks disappointed

suppress silence, restrain

on the spot right at that moment

I'm going to die I'm very embarrassed

Because they're clapping for you, that's why, and whoever heard of dying while they're clapping for you? And they're smiling at you. People who never even *saw* you before are smiling at you and slapping your back and pumping your hand, and suddenly it seems like the whole world is calling your name, and you're feeling so good you pretty much just float on home from school. And when you go to bed that night, the last thing you see before you **zonk out** are those eyes, and the last thing on your face is a smile.

Or maybe you showed up at school with really unusual earrings. Or you **aced a test**. Or broke your arm. Or got your braces off. Or maybe you weren't even a person. Maybe you were a charcoal drawing on the wall done by an art whiz. Or a really neat-looking bug out by the bike rack.

We wagged our heads and agreed what a goofy girl this was, maybe even officially crazy, but we walked away smiling and maybe not saying but all thinking the same thing: it felt good to **get credit**.

And if this had been any other year, things might have just gone on and on like that. But this was the year something unbelievable was happening on the basketball court. This was the year the team was winning. *Only* winning.

And that changed everything.

Early in the season no one noticed. Except for girls' tennis, we had never had good teams in anything. We expected to lose. We were comfortable with losing. In fact, most of us were

....

zonk out fall asleep
aced a test got an A on a test
get credit be praised; be noticed

oblivious to it, since we didn't even attend the games.

The year before, the basketball Electrons had won only five of twenty-six games. This year, they won their fifth game before Christmas. By early January they had won the tenth, and people began to notice that there was still a zero in the loss column.

"UNDEFEATED!" blared a sign on the plywood roadrunner. Some said we were winning by accident. Some said the other teams were simply more rotten than we were. Some thought the sign was a joke. One thing was certain: attendance went up. By the start of February the winning streak had reached sixteen, and there wasn't an empty seat in the gym.

But something even more interesting was happening. Suddenly we were no longer comfortable with losing. **In fact, we forgot how to lose.** The transformation was stunning in its speed. There was no apprenticeship period, no learning curve. No one had to teach us how to be winners. One day we were bored, indifferent, satisfied losers; the next we were **rabid fanatics**, stomping in the grandstand, painting our faces green and white, doing the wave as if we had been perfecting it for years.

We fell in love with our team. When we spoke of it, we used the word "we" instead of "they." The leading scorer, Brent Ardsley, seemed to have a golden glow about him as he moved through the school. And the more we loved our team, the more we hated the opposition. We used to envy them. We even applauded them to spite our own hapless teams.

···

oblivious to not aware of

In fact, we forgot how to lose. We acted like we had never lost a game before.

rabid fanatics very excited fans

Now we **detested the opposition** and everything about them. We hated their uniforms. We hated their coaches and their fans. We hated them because they were trying to spoil our perfect season. We resented every point scored against us. And how dare they celebrate!

We began to boo. It was our first experience as booers, but you'd have thought we **were veterans**. We booed the other team, we booed the other coach, we booed the other fans, the referees—whatever threatened our perfect season, we booed it.

We even booed the scoreboard. We hated games that **went down to the wire**. We hated suspense. We loved games that were decided in the first five minutes. We wanted more than victories, we wanted **massacres**. The only score we would have been totally happy with would have been 100 to 0.

And right there in the middle of it all, in the midst of this perfect season mania, was Stargirl, popping up whenever the ball went through the net, no matter which team scored, cheering everything and everybody. It was sometime in January when calls started flying from the stands: "Siddown!" Then came the boos. She didn't seem to notice.

She did not seem to notice.

Of all the unusual features of Stargirl, this struck me as the most remarkable. **Bad things did not stick to her.** Correction: *her* bad things did not stick to her. *Our* bad things stuck very much to her. If we were hurt, if we were unhappy or otherwise victimized by life, she seemed to know about it, and to care, as soon as we did. But bad things falling on her—unkind words,

....

detested the opposition hated the other team
were veterans had been doing it for a long time
went down to the wire had close scores right to the end
massacres to win by a lot of points
Bad things did not stick to her. She did not notice bad things.

nasty stares, foot blisters—she seemed unaware of. I never saw her look in a mirror, never heard her complain. All of her feelings, all of her attentions flowed outward. **She had no ego.**

The nineteenth game of the basketball season was played at Red Rock. In previous years cheerleaders had outnumbered Mica fans at away games. Not now. The convoy rolling across the desert that evening stretched for a couple of miles. By the time we were seated, there was barely room for the home-team fans.

It was the worst slaughter of the year. Red Rock was helpless. By the start of the fourth quarter we were ahead, 78 to 29. The coach put in the subs. We booed. We smelled a hundred points. **We wanted blood.** The coach put the starters back in. As we howled and thundered in the stands, Stargirl got up and walked from the gym. Those of us who noticed assumed she was going to the rest room. I kept glancing toward the exit. She never returned. With five seconds left in the game, the Electrons scored the hundredth point. We went nuts.

Stargirl had been outside the whole time, chatting with the bus driver. The other cheerleaders asked her why she left. She said she felt sorry for the Red Rock players. She felt her cheering was only making the massacre worse. Such games were no fun, she said. Your job isn't to have fun, they told her, your job is to cheer for Mica High no matter what. She just stared at them.

The team and the cheerleaders rode the same bus. When the players came out from the locker room, the cheerleaders

....

She had no ego. She was more concerned about others than herself.

We wanted blood. We wanted to win badly.

told them what had happened. They **devised** a trick. They told Stargirl that someone had forgotten something in the gym, and would she please go get it. With Stargirl gone, they told the bus driver everyone was aboard, and the bus **made the two-hour return trip** without her.

A Red Rock custodian drove her home that night. Next day in school, the cheerleaders told her it was all a big misunderstanding and acted as if they were sorry. She believed them.

The next day was February thirteenth. The Hot Seat.

....

devised planned

made the two-hour return trip went back to Mica High

12

This is how *Hot Seat* went.

It took place in the communications center studio. There were two chairs on stage: the infamous Hot Seat itself—painted red with flames running up the legs—and an ordinary chair for the host, Kevin. Off to the side were two rows of six chairs each, the second row higher than the first. This was where the jury sat.

It was a jury in name only. The twelve members did not vote or **render a verdict**. Their job was to ask questions, to give the Hot Seat its heat: ticklish questions, embarrassing questions, nosy questions. But not mean or hurtful questions. The idea was to make the subject **squirm, not roast**.

In the spirit of mock inquisition, we called the subject the "victim." And why would anyone want to be the victim? The lure of TV. The chance to confess—or lie—before a camera and before peers instead of parents. But I doubted the usual reasons applied to Stargirl.

There were three cameras: one for the stage, one for the jury, and Chico. Chico was the handheld close-up camera. According to Mr. Robineau, our faculty advisor, a student named Chico once begged him to be a close-up camera kid. Mr. Robineau gave him a tryout, but Chico was so skinny he practically collapsed under the camera. The job went to someone else and Chico went to the weight room. By the

....

render a verdict decide if someone was guilty or innocent

squirm, not roast feel embarrassed, not attacked

In the spirit of mock inquisition To pretend we were attacking following year Chico had muscles, and the camera was like nothing on his shoulder. He got the job, and he was brilliant at it. He gave the camera his own name. "We are one," he said. When he graduated, his name stayed behind, and from then on the close-up camera and its operator were a unit called Chico.

The host and the victim were each **fitted with a thimble-size clip-on mike**; the jury passed around a hand mike. Opposite the stage was the glassed-in control room, sound-insulated from the rest of the studio. That's where I worked, wearing my headset, watching the monitors, directing the shots. I stood at the shoulder of the technical director, or TD. He sat at a rack of buttons, **punching up the shots I ordered**. Also in the control room were the graphics and audio people. Mr. Robineau was there as faculty overseer, but basically the students worked everything.

Kevin's job was to get things started: intro the victim, ask a few opening questions, stir things up if the jury was slow. Usually the jury was **on the ball**. Typical questions: "Does it bother you that you're so short?" "Is it true that you like so-and-so?" "Do you wish you were good-looking?" "How often do you take a shower?"

It almost always added up to entertainment. At the end of the half hour, as we cued credits and music, there was always a good feeling in the air, and everyone—victim, jury members, studio crew—mingled and became students again.

We filmed the shows after school, then broadcast them that night—prime time—on local cable. About ten thousand homes.

....

fitted with a thimble-size clip-on mike given a small microphone to attach to their clothes

punching up the shots I ordered pressing buttons to change the view of the camera

on the ball ready with good questions

Our own surveys said at least fifty percent of the student body watched any given show. We **outdrew** most of the hot sitcoms. We expected to top ninety percent for the Stargirl show.

But I had a secret: I wished no one would watch.

In the month since we had scheduled the show, **Stargirl's popularity had dropped out of sight**. Gone were ukuleles from the lunchroom. More and more kids saw her cheerleading behavior as **undermining** the basketball team and its perfect record. I was afraid the boos for her might spread from the court to the studio. I was afraid the show might turn ugly.

When Stargirl came in that day after school, Kevin gave her the usual briefing while Mr. Robineau and I checked out the equipment. As the jury members straggled in, they were not clowning around or tap-dancing on the stage as jurors usually did. They went right to their seats. Stargirl was the one tap-dancing. And mugging for the cameras with Cinnamon the rat licking her nose. Kevin was cracking up, but the faces of the jurors were grim. One of them was Hillari Kimble. My bad feeling got worse.

I retreated to the control room and shut the door. I checked communications with the cameras. We were ready. Kevin and Stargirl took their seats. I took one last look through the plate glass that separated the set from the control room. For the next half hour I would see the world through four monitors. "Okay, everybody," I announced, "here we go." I cut the studio mike. I looked over my control-room mates. "We all set?"

....

outdrew had more viewers than
Stargirl's popularity had dropped out of sight Stargirl had quit being popular
undermining hurting

Everyone nodded.

Just then Stargirl lifted one of Cinnamon's front paws and waved it at the control room and said in a squeaky voice, "Hi, Leo."

I froze. **I came unraveled.** I didn't know she knew my name. I just stood there like a dummy. Finally I waggled my fingers at the rat and mouthed the words "Hi, Cinnamon," although they couldn't hear me on the other side of the glass.

I took a deep breath. "Okay, ready music, ready intro." I paused. "Music, intro."

This was the moment I lived for, launching the show. I was the director, the maestro, I called the shots. On the monitors before me I watched the program unfold according to my commands. But on this day the thrill was missing. I felt only **a dark dread snaking along the cables.**

"Greetings . . . and welcome to *Hot Seat* . . . "

Kevin went through the opening **spiel.** Kevin loved to be on camera. He was ideal for a show like this, which made good use of his smirky grin and arching, Did-I-really-hear-you-say-that? eyebrows.

He turned to Stargirl. Then, **impromptu,** he reached out and stroked the nose of Cinnamon, who was perched on Stargirl's shoulder. "Want to hold him?" she said.

Kevin gave the camera a Should-I look. "Sure," he said.

"Ready, Chico, rat," I said into my headset mike.

"Ready" was always first in the command sequence. Chico zoomed in.

....

I came unraveled. I could not think.

a dark dread snaking along the cables something bad

spiel speech, routine

impromptu even though he had not planned it

69

"Chico."

TD punched up Chico. The camera followed Cinnamon from Stargirl's hands to Kevin's. No sooner was the rat in Kevin's lap than it scampered up his chest and darted between two buttons into his shirt. Kevin yipped and squirmed. "It scratches!"

"He has fingernails," Stargirl said calmly. "He won't hurt you."

Chico **nailed** Cinnamon poking his head out from between the two buttons. Mr. Robineau stuck a thumbs-up in front of my face.

Kevin gave the camera his Ain't-I-something face. He turned again to Stargirl. "You know, ever since you showed up at school this year, we've been wanting to put you on the Hot Seat."

Stargirl stared at him. She turned to the live camera. Her eyes were growing wider . . .

Something was happening.

. . . and wider . . .

"Chico!" I barked.

Chico moved in, crouching, **giving it a little upshot**. Terrific. "Closer, closer," I said.

Stargirl's wonderstruck eyes practically filled the screen. I checked the long-shot monitor. She was frozen, rigid, as if **electrified** to the chair.

Someone smacked my shoulder. I turned. Mr. Robineau was laughing, saying something. I lifted one earphone. "She's

....

nailed got a perfect picture of

giving it a little upshot pointing the camera up at Stargirl

electrified stuck

joking," he repeated. And suddenly I saw. **She was taking "Hot Seat" literally.** She was **milking it for all it was worth,** and judging from the blank stares of Kevin and the jury, Mr. Robineau and I were the only ones who got the joke.

Stargirl's hands were rising now from the arms of the Hot Seat . . .

"Ready one," I called. "One!"

Camera One, not there at first but getting it now, the long shot, nailing her as her hands came off the chair arms, fingers spread wide, you could almost see her fingertips smoking . . .

Hold it, I prayed, *hold it . . .*

. . . as her horrified eyes swung down over the side of the chair, the Hot Seat, saw the painted flames . . .

"EEEEEEEEEEEEYIKES!"

Her scream bent instrument dials like palms in a hurricane. The rat leaped from Kevin's shirt. The TV image quaked as my Camera One man flinched, but he recovered and caught her standing now on the front edge of the stage, bending over with her rear end in the camera, flapping her hand behind her, **fanning her smoking fanny.**

Finally Kevin got it. He went nuts.

"One, pull back, get Kevin in it. Ready . . . One."

Kevin was doubled up, tipping out of his chair, on his knees on the stage. His laughter flooded the control room. The rat ran over his hands and hopped down the single stage step . . .

"The rat!" I yelled. "Two, get the rat!"

But Two couldn't get the rat because the rat was nosing

....

She was taking "Hot Seat" literally. She was pretending that the "Hot Seat" actually was hot.

milking it for all it was worth acting funny

fanning her smoking fanny pretending her bottom had been burned

71

around Two's feet and Two was bolting from his camera.

"Chico, rat!"

Chico dived. He was flat on the floor, **feeding** the live screen a brilliant shot of the rat heading over to the jury, the jury members scrambling, taking off, climbing onto their seats.

Forget the "Readys"; things were happening too fast. The cameras were **dancing**, feeding the monitors. I barked commands. TD was punching his button rack like some hard-rock keyboarder.

Stargirl's pantomime remains the best I have ever seen. Mr. Robineau kept squeezing my shoulder. As he said later, it was the greatest moment in Hot Seat history.

But because of what followed, no audience would ever see it.

....

feeding giving

Forget the "Readys" I didn't have time to say "Ready" before I made a command

dancing moving all around

BEFORE YOU MOVE ON...

1. **Conclusions** Reread pages 64–65. Why do the students trick Stargirl at the game?

2. **Predict** Reread page 72. How will *Hot Seat* end? How do you know?

LOOK AHEAD Read pages 73–86 to find out how the *Hot Seat* jury will judge Stargirl.

13

In less than a minute, everything returned to normal. Stargirl retrieved Cinnamon and sat back coolly in the Hot Seat as if nothing had happened. **Kevin's eyes twinkled.** He was squirming. He couldn't wait to **dig into the interview.** Neither could the jury, but their eyes were not twinkling.

Kevin forced himself to look serious. "So, your name. Stargirl. It's pretty unusual."

Stargirl gave him a blank look.

Kevin was **flustered.** "Isn't it?" he said.

Stargirl shrugged, "Not to me."

She's **putting him on,** I thought. "Chico," I said into my mike, "stay tight on her face."

A voice was heard dimly off-camera. Kevin turned. A jury member had spoken. "Jury mike up," I said. "Ready Two." The mike was passed to Jennifer St. John. "Two."

The mike looked like a black ice cream cone before Jennifer's face. Her voice wasn't pleasant. "What was wrong with the name your parents gave you?"

Stargirl turned slowly to Jennifer. She smiled. "Nothing. It was a good name."

"What was it?"

"Susan."

"So why did you drop it?"

"Because I didn't feel like Susan anymore."

....

Kevin's eyes twinkled. Kevin was excited.
dig into the interview ask Stargirl questions
flustered suddenly nervous
putting him on teasing him

"So you just threw out Susan and named yourself Stargirl."

"No." Still smiling.

"No?"

"Pocket Mouse."

Twelve pairs of eyes boggled.

"What?"

"I named myself Pocket Mouse," Stargirl said **breezily.** "Then Mudpie. Then Hullygully. *Then* Stargirl."

Damon Ricci snatched the mike from Jennifer St. John. "So what's it gonna be next? Dog Turd?"

Uh-oh, I thought, *here we go.*

Kevin jumped in. "So . . . you change your name whenever you get tired of it?"

"Whenever it doesn't fit anymore. I'm not my name. My name is something I wear, like a shirt. It gets worn, I outgrow it, I change it."

"So why Stargirl?"

"Oh, I don't know." She petted Cinnamon's nose with her fingertip. "I was walking in the desert one night, looking up at the sky—like," she chuckled, "how can you *not* look at the sky! —and it just sort of came to me, **fell onto me.**"

Kevin looked up from his sheet of prepared questions. "So what do your parents think? Are they sad you didn't keep Susan?"

"No. It was almost their idea. When I started calling myself Pocket Mouse when I was little, they called me that, too. And we just never went back."

....

Twelve pairs of eyes boggled. Everyone looked very surprised.

breezily casually; without embarrassment

fell onto me it felt like a perfect name

Another distant voice from the jury.

I tapped the soundman. "Jury mike. And keep all mikes **open**." I hated to do it.

It was Mike Ebersole. "I said, do you love your country?"

"Yes," she answered briskly. "Do you love yours?"

Ebersole ignored her question. "Why don't you say the Pledge of Allegiance right?"

She smiled. "Sounds right to me."

"Sounds like **you're a traitor to me**."

Jurors were only supposed to ask questions, not make statements.

A hand **reached into the picture** and grabbed the mike from Ebersole. Becca Rinaldi's angry face appeared on Camera Two. "Why do you cheer for the other team?"

Stargirl seemed to be thinking it over. "I guess because I'm a cheerleader."

"You're not *just* a cheerleader, you **dumb cluck**"—Becca Rinaldi was snarling into the mike—"you're supposed to be *our* cheerleader. A *Mica* cheerleader."

I glanced at Mr. Robineau. He was turned away from the monitors. He was staring straight at the set through the control room window.

Stargirl was leaning forward, looking earnestly at Becca Rinaldi, her voice small as a little girl's. "When the other team scores a point and you see how happy it makes all their fans, doesn't it make you happy, too?"

Becca growled, "No."

....

open on; ready to be used

you're a traitor to me you hate your country

reached into the picture was seen by the camera

dumb cluck stupid girl

"Doesn't it make you want to join in?"

"No."

"Don't you ever want the other team to be happy, too?"

"No."

Stargirl seemed **genuinely** surprised. "You don't always want to be the winner . . . do you?"

Becca scowled at her, **jutted out her jaw**. "Yes. Yes, I do. Yes. I *always* want to be the winner. That's what I do. I **root** for us to win. That's what we all do." She swept her arm around the set. "We root for Mica." She jabbed her finger at the stage. "Who do you root for?"

Stargirl hesitated. She smiled, she threw out her arms. "I root for *everybody!*"

Kevin—to the rescue, thankfully—clapped his hands. "Hey—how about this? Maybe it should be official. Maybe one person in the whole district should he appointed to be on"—he waved his arm—"everybody's side!"

Stargirl reached over and slapped Kevin's knee. "She could wear **every school's letter** on her sweater!"

Kevin laughed. "She'd have to be big as a house!"

Stargirl slapped her own knee. "Then no letter at all. That's even better." She looked into the camera, she swiped at the space before her, "Out with letters!"

"Cheerleader-at-large!"

"Everybody's cheerleader!"

Kevin sat at attention, placed his hand over his heart. "With liberty and justice . . . and a cheerleader for all."

....

genuinely truly, honestly

jutted out her jaw looking mean

root cheer

every school's letter letters to represent every school

Ebersole snarled into the jury mike: "And a **nut roll** for all."

Kevin wagged his finger. "That's a no-no," he scolded. "No statements from the jury. Questions only."

Renee Bozeman snatched the mike. "Okay, here's a question. Why did you quit homeschooling?"

Stargirl's face became serious. "I wanted to make friends."

"Well, you sure have a funny way of showing it, making the whole school mad at you."

I wished I had never given in to Hot-Seating Stargirl.

Stargirl just stared. Chico filled the screen with her face.

"Gimme—" It was Jennifer St. John, reaching for the mike. "And out of school, too. You **meddle into** everybody's business. You **stick your nose in**, whether you're invited or not. Why do you do that?"

Stargirl had no reply. Her usual **impish** expression was gone. She looked at Jennifer. She looked at the camera, as if trying to find an answer in the lens. Then she was looking away, looking at the control room. I took my eyes from the monitor and for a second I thought they met hers at the control room window.

I had been wondering when Hillari Kimble would speak up. Now she did. "I'm gonna tell you something, girl. You're goofy. You're crazy." Hillari was standing, jabbing her finger at Stargirl, chewing on the mike. "You must've come from Mars or something . . ." Kevin raised a timid hand. "And don't you tell me 'no statements,' Kevin. Where'd you come from, Mars or something? There, now it's a question. Why don't you go

....

nut roll crazy person
meddle into become involved with
stick your nose in become involved
impish playful

back to where you came from? There's another question."

Stargirl's eyes filled the camera. *Don't cry*, I prayed.

There was no stopping Hillari. "You want to cheer for other schools? Fine! Go there! Don't come to *my* school. Get outta *my* school!"

Other hands were **snatching at** the mike.

"I know what your problem is. All this weird stuff you do? It's just to get attention."

"It's to get a boyfriend!"

The jurors laughed. They were a mob. Hands grabbed at the mike. Kevin looked anxiously at me. I could do nothing. With all the buttons and switches at my command, I was helpless to change anything on the other side of the glass.

"I got a simple question for you. What's the matter with you? Huh? *Huh?*"

"Why can't you be normal?"

"Why do you wanna be so different?"

"Yeah—is something wrong with us, you gotta be so different?"

"Why don't you wear makeup?"

They were all standing now, jabbing, jutting, shouting, whether they had the mike or not.

"You don't like us, do you? *Do* you?"

Mr. Robineau **flipped the master toggle on the console**. "That's it," he said.

I flipped the studio sound switch. "That's it. Show's over."

The jury went on shouting.

....

snatching at trying to get

flipped the master toggle on the console stopped the show

I flipped the studio sound switch. I turned off the microphones and speakers.

14

This was the start of a period that blurs as I try to recall it.
Incidents seem to cascade and merge. Events become
feelings, feelings become events. **Head and heart are contrary
historians.**

The *Hot Seat* session was never aired. Mr. Robineau
destroyed the tape. Of course, that didn't stop every moment
of it from being reported. In fact, most of the students knew
about it by the time school opened next day.

What I recall then, when the last detail had been spilled,
is a period of whispers and waiting. Tension. What would
happen now? Would the jury's **open hostility spill over into**
the classrooms? How would Stargirl react? Answers were
expected on the following day, Valentine's Day. On previous
holidays—Halloween, Thanksgiving, Christmas, Groundhog
Day—Stargirl had left a little something on each desk in her
homeroom. Would she do likewise this time?

The answer was yes. Each member of Homeroom 17 found
a candy heart on his or her desk that morning.

There was a basketball game that night; that I do remember.
The biggest game of the year. The Electrons had breezed
through the regular season undefeated, but now the second
season was about to begin: the play-offs. First the districts, then
the regionals, and finally the state tournament. We had never

....

Incidents seem to cascade and merge. I can't remember
exactly what happened.

Head and heart are contrary historians. Emotions can
change memories.

open hostility spill over into anger be repeated in

even made it to the districts, but now visions of championships danced in our heads. The Electrons—champions of all Arizona! We would settle for nothing less.

First hurdle in our way was Sun Valley, champions of the Pima League. The game was played Valentine's night on a neutral court in Casa Grande. All of Mica, it seemed, emptied out and headed for the game. Kevin and I went in the pickup.

From the moment the Mica mob entered the gym, our cheers **rattled the rafters**. The big green M on Stargirl's white sweater flounced as she spun and leaped with the other cheerleaders. I spent as much time watching her as I did watching the game. She cheered when we scored. When Sun Valley scored, she did not. Something inside me felt better.

But not for long. We were losing. For the first time all year, we were trailing at the end of the first quarter. In fact, we were **getting smoked**, 21 to 9. The reason was no mystery. While Sun Valley's team was not as good as ours, they did have one thing we did not: a superstar. A kid named Ron Kovac. He stood six-foot-eight and averaged thirty points per game. Our players looked like **five Davids flailing against Goliath**.

Sun Valley's lead had increased to nineteen points midway through the second quarter. Our once-raucous fans were stunned into silence, and that's when it happened. The ball was loose in the middle of the floor. Several players from each team dived for it. At that moment Kovac was running past, trying to avoid the divers, and his right foot came down on a prone player's sneaker—so it was told in the newspapers the

....

rattled the rafters were really loud

getting smoked losing badly

five Davids flailing against Goliath five weaker players fighting against one great player next day. At the time, it happened so fast no one saw it, though several people said they heard a **sickening crack**, like a twig snapping. All we knew was that suddenly Goliath was on the floor writhing and screaming, and his right foot looked all wrong, and the Sun Valley coaches and trainer and players were sprinting across the floor. But they were not the first. Stargirl, somehow, was already there.

While Kovac's own cheerleaders sat gaping and **stricken** on their bench, Stargirl knelt on the hardwood floor. She held his head in her lap while the others attended his broken leg. Her hands moved over his face and forehead. She seemed to be saying things to him. When they carried him away on a stretcher, she followed. Everyone—both sides—stood and applauded. The Sun Valley cheerleaders leaped as if he had just scored two points. Ambulance lights flashed in the high windows.

I knew why I was applauding, but I wondered about some of the other Mica fans. Were they really standing **in tribute**, or because they were happy to see him go?

The game resumed. Stargirl returned to the cheerleaders' bench. Without Kovac, Sun Valley was **a pushover**. By early in the second half we took the lead and went on to win easily.

Two nights later we lost to Glendale. Again we fell farther and farther behind as the first half went on. But this time there was no turnaround in the second half. This time the Electrons faced not one but five players better than themselves. This time no opponent broke an ankle, though I'm sure in our desperation

....

sickening crack terrible breaking sound
stricken scared
in tribute to honor Kovac
a pushover easy to beat

81

some of us secretly wished for it.

We were shocked. We couldn't believe it. And then, as the seconds of the fourth quarter ticked by, we did believe. The cheers from across the gym **were like volleys of arrows piercing our grand delusion**. How could we have been so stupid? Did we really think that little Mica, undefeated in its own third-rate league, could ever stand up to the big-city powerhouses around the state? We had been lured into great, foolish expectations. Suckered. We were devastated. It had been so wonderful to be winners. And so right for us. Winning, we had come to believe, was our destiny.

And now . . .

As the Glendale coach sent in the **scrubs to mop us up**, Mica girls wept. Boys cursed and booed. Some blamed the officials. Or the nets. Or the lights. The cheerleaders, to their credit, kept on cheering. They looked up at us with glistening eyes and mascara tracks on their cheeks. They pumped their arms and shouted and did everything that cheerleaders are supposed to do, but their gestures were empty, **their hearts not in it**.

Except for Stargirl. As I watched her intently, I could see that she was different. Her cheeks were dry. There was no crack in her voice, no sag in her shoulders. From the start of the second half on, she never sat down. And she never again looked at the game. She turned her back on the court. She stood and faced us and gave not an ounce of herself to the jubilation across the gym. We were losing by thirty points with a minute to go,

....

were like volleys of arrows piercing our grand delusion made us realize we were really going to lose

scrubs to mop us up players that would end the game

their hearts not in it they did not believe we could win.

but she cheered on as if we had a chance. **Her eyes blazed with a ferocity** I had never seen before. She shook her fists at us. **She flung her defiance at our gloom.**

And then her face was bloody.

A Glendale player had just dunked the ball and Kevin pounded my knee with his fist and I looked to see Stargirl's face suddenly a bloody mask and I was on my feet screaming, "NOOOOO!"

But it wasn't blood. It was a tomato. Someone had splattered her face with a perfectly thrown ripe tomato, and as the clock expired and the Glendale fans poured onto the court, Stargirl just stood there, her great eyes staring up at us **in utter bewilderment through the pulpy red gore**. Spouts of bitter laughter erupted among us, even some applause.

The next morning at home I found the card. It was in a school notebook that apparently I had not opened for several days. It was a valentine, one of those little cut-out third-grade sorts, showing a blushing little boy and a girl with mary jane shoes and a big red heart between them and the words "I LOVE YOU." And as third-graders—and highschoolers—often do, the sender had signed it in code:

....

Her eyes blazed with a ferocity She showed a determination

She flung her defiance at our gloom. She tried to cheer us up.

in utter bewilderment through the pulpy red gore with confusion through the tomato juice

15

She gave everybody in school a card. That was my first thought.

When I saw Kevin at school, I was about to ask him, but I **pulled back**. I waited until lunch. I tried to be casual. I slipped it in with the only thing that mattered that day. The school was **in mourning**. The game. The loss. The tomato. Oh yeah, incidentally, speaking of Stargirl: "Did you happen to get a card?"

He looked at me funny. "She gave them to her homeroom, I heard."

"Yeah," I said, "that's what I heard, too. But was that all? Didn't she give them to everybody else?"

He shrugged. "Not to me. Why? You get one?"

He was looking away across the lunchroom, biting into his sandwich, yet I felt he was **grilling me**. I shook my head. "Oh no, just wondering."

Actually, I was sitting on the card. It was in the back pocket of my jeans. Meanwhile, all eyes in the lunchroom were on Stargirl. I think we half expected to see traces of red still clinging to her face. She sat at her usual table with Dori Dilson and several other friends. She seemed **subdued**. She did not play her ukulele. She did not play with her rat. She just ate and talked with the girls at her table.

As the lunch period was ending, she got up but did not head

....

pulled back stopped
in mourning very sad, as if someone died
grilling me asking me too many questions
subdued quiet, sad

straight for the exit. Instead she detoured in the direction of my table. I panicked. I jumped up, grabbed my stuff, **blurted** "Gotta go," left Kevin with his mouth hanging, and took off. Not fast enough. Halfway to the door I heard her behind me: "Hi, Leo." My face got warm. I was sure every eye was turned to me. I was sure they could all see the card in my pocket. I pretended to look at the clock, I pretended I was late for something. I ran from the lunchroom.

I **lurked in the shadows** for the rest of the day. I went straight home after school. I stayed in my room. I came out only for dinner. I told my parents I had a project to do. I paced. I lay on my bed and stared at the ceiling. I stared out the window. I laid the card on my study desk. I picked it up. I read it. I read it. I read it. I played "Hi, Leo" over and over in my head. I tossed darts at the corkboard on the back of my door. My father called in, "What's your project, darts?" I went out. I drove around in the pickup. I drove down her street. At the last intersection before her house, I **turned off**.

For hours I lay **under my sheet of moonlight**. Her voice came through the night, from the light, from the stars.

Hi, Leo.

In the morning—it was a Saturday—Kevin and I went together to Archie's for the weekly meeting of the Loyal Order of the Stone Bone. There were about fifteen of us. We wore our fossil necklaces. Archie wanted to discuss the Eocene skull he was holding, but all the others could talk about was the game.

....

blurted said quickly
lurked in the shadows tried to hide
turned off turned to go down a different street
under my sheet of moonlight on my bed in the moonlight

When they told Archie about the tomato, his eyebrows went up, but other than that, his face did not change. I thought, *This is not news to him, he already knows.*

Archie spent the whole session that way, nodding and smiling and raising his eyebrows. We dumped our disappointment on him, the devastation of the loss. He said very little. When it was over, he looked down at the skull in his lap and patted it and said, "Well, this fellow here lost his game, too. He was winning for ten million years or so, but then the early grasses started growing up around him, and he found **himself in a different league**. He hung in there as well as he could. He scored his points, but he kept falling farther and farther behind. The opposition was better, quicker, keener. In the championship game, our boy got **annihilated**. Not only didn't he show up for class the next day, he never showed up, period. They never saw him again."

Archie lifted the snouted, fox-size skull until it was side by side with his own face. A good minute passed as he said nothing, inviting us into our own thoughts. **Faces staring at faces staring at faces.** Tens of millions of years of faces in a living room in a place called Arizona.

....

himself in a different league that he could not compete

annihilated beaten badly

Faces staring at faces staring at faces. We just stared at each other's faces.

BEFORE YOU MOVE ON...

1. **Inference** Reread page 78. What are the real reasons the jury is angry with Stargirl?

2. **Metaphor** Reread page 86. Why does Archie compare his fossil to a basketball player?

LOOK AHEAD Read pages 87–106. Does Leo love Stargirl?

16

Monday. Lunch.

This time I stayed put when Stargirl came toward my table
on her way out. My back was to her. I could see Kevin's eyes
following her, widening as she came closer. And then his eyes
stopped, and his mouth was **sliding toward a wicked grin**, and
it seemed like everything stopped but the clink of pans in the
kitchen, and the back of my neck was on fire.

"You're welcome," I heard her say, almost sing.

I thought, *What?* but then I knew what. And I knew what
I had to do. I knew I had to turn around and speak to her, and
I knew she was going to stand there until I did. This was silly,
this was childish, this being terrified of her. What was I afraid
of, anyway?

I turned. I felt heavy, as if I were moving through water, as
if I were confronting much more than a tenth-grade girl with
an unusual name. I faced the gaudy sunflower on her canvas
bag—it looked hand-painted—and at last my eyes fell into hers.
I said, "Thanks for the card."

Her smile **put the sunflower to shame**. She walked off.

Kevin was grinning, wagging his head. "She's in love."

"**Bull**," I said.

"She is mucho in love."

"She's goofy, that's all."

The bell rang. We gathered our stuff and left.

....

sliding toward a wicked grin smiling like he knew a secret
put the sunflower to shame was beautiful
Bull That is not true

I **wobbled through** the rest of the day. A baseball bat could not have hit me harder than that smile did. I was sixteen years old. In that time, how many thousands of smiles had been aimed at me? So why did this one feel like the first?

After school my feet carried me toward her homeroom. I was trembling. **My stomach had flies.** I had no idea what I was going to do if I saw her. I only knew I couldn't *not go.*

She wasn't there. I hurried through the hallways. I ran outside. The buses were loading. Cars were revving. Hundreds of kids were scattering. For months she had been everywhere, now she was nowhere.

I heard her name. *Her name.* The same two syllables, the same eight letters that I had been hearing all year, and suddenly the sound struck my ear with a *ping* of pure silver. I drifted sideways to overhear. A group of girls was chattering toward a bus.

"When?"

"Today. After school. Just now!"

"I don't believe it!"

"I don't believe it took so long."

"**Kicked off?** Are they allowed?"

"Sure. Why not? It's not *her* school."

"I would've kicked her off long ago. It was treason."

"**Good riddance.**"

I knew what they were talking about. It had been rumored for days. Stargirl had been kicked off the cheerleading squad.

"Hi, Leo!"

....

wobbled through had trouble concentrating

My stomach had flies. I was nervous.

Kicked off? Made her quit?

"Good Riddance." "I am glad."

A chorus of girl voices calling my name. I turned. They were in front of the sun. I shaded my eyes. They sang in unison: "Starboy!" They laughed. I waved and hurried home. I could never have admitted it, but I was thrilled.

Her house was two miles from mine, behind a little ten-store shopping center. Archie had told me where. I walked. I didn't want to ride. I wanted to be slow about it. I wanted to feel myself getting closer step by step, feel the tension rising like fizz in a soda bottle.

I did not know what I would do if I saw her. I knew only that I was nervous, afraid. **I was more comfortable with her as history than as person.** Suddenly, intensely, I wanted to know everything about her. I wanted to see her baby pictures. I wanted to watch her eating breakfast, wrapping a gift, sleeping. Since September she had been a performer—unique and outrageous—on the high school stage. She was the opposite of cool; she **held nothing back**. From her decorated desk to her oratorical speech to her performance on the football field, she was there for all to see. And yet now I felt I had not been paying attention. I felt I had missed something, something important.

She lived on Palo Verde. For a person so different, her house was surprisingly ordinary, at least by Arizona standards. Single story. Pale adobe. Clay-red pipetile roof. Not a blade of grass in the small front yard, but rather barrel and prickly pear cacti and clusters of stones.

It was dark, as I had intended, when I got there. I walked

....

I was more comfortable with her as history than as person. It was easier to think about her than talk to her.

held nothing back shared everything about herself

up and down the other side of the street. It occurred to me I might be mistaken for a **prowler**, so I walked around the block. I stopped into Roma Delite for a slice of pizza. Gulped down only half of it, hurried back out, couldn't relax when her house was not in sight. Couldn't relax when it was.

At first it was enough just to see the house. Then I began to wonder if she was inside. I wondered what she could be doing. Light came from every window I could see. There was a car in the driveway. The longer I hung around, the closer I wanted to be. I crossed the street and practically dashed past the house. As I went by, I scooped up a stone from the yard. I went up the street, turned, and looked at her house in the distance.

I whispered to the **salt-sprinkled** sky, "That's where Stargirl Caraway lives. She likes me."

I headed back toward the house. The street, the sidewalks were deserted. The stone was warm in my hand. This time I walked slowly as I approached. I felt strange. My eyes fixed on a triangle of light in a curtained window. I saw a shadow on a yellow wall. I seemed to be **drifting, footless**, into the light.

Suddenly the front door opened. I dived behind the car in the driveway and crouched by the rear fender. I heard the door close. I heard steps. The steps matched the movement of a long shadow **cast down** the driveway. My breath stopped. The shadow stopped. I felt both ridiculous and weirdly, perfectly placed, as if crouching by that car was precisely what life had in store for me at that moment.

Her voice came from beyond the shadow. "Remember when

....

prowler criminal
salt-sprinkled star-filled
drifting, footless floating
cast down that was on

you followed me into the desert that day after school?"

Absurdly, I debated whether to answer, as if doing so would—what? **Give me away?** I leaned into the smooth metal of the fender. It never occurred to me to stand, to show myself. Hours seemed to pass before I finally croaked, "Yes."

"Why did you turn around and go back?"

Her tone was casual, as if she held conversations every night with people crouching behind the car in the driveway.

"I don't remember," I said.

"Were you afraid?"

"No," I lied.

"I wouldn't have let you get lost, you know."

"I know."

A little shadow **detached** itself from the larger one. It came toward me, wavering over the pebbled driveway. It had a tail. It wasn't a shadow. It was the rat, Cinnamon. Cinnamon stopped at the tip of one of my sneakers. He stood, looking up at me. He put his front paws on top of my sneaker and nosed into the laces.

"Are you getting **acquainted with** Cinnamon?"

"Sort of."

"Are you lying?"

"Sort of."

"Are you afraid of rats?"

"Sort of."

"Do you think I'm cute? If you say sort of, I'll tell Cinnamon to bite you."

....

Give me away? Show that I was hiding?
detached separated
acquainted with to know

"Yes."

"Yes, what?"

"I think you're cute." I thought of adding "sort of" just to be funny, but I didn't.

"Do you think Cinnamon is cute?"

The rat had climbed fully onto my sneaker now. I could feel his weight. I wanted to shake him off. His tail spilled onto the driveway. "**No comment**," I said.

"Oh my, hear that, Cinnamon? No comment. He doesn't want people to know he thinks you're cute."

"I think you're **getting a little carried away**," I said.

"I certainly hope so," she said. "Nothing's more fun than being carried away. Would you like to carry Cinnamon away for the night? He loves **sleep-overs**."

"No thank you."

"Oh." **Her voice was mock-pouty.** "Are you sure? He's no trouble. He hardly takes up any room. All you have to feed him is a Mini Wheat. Or two grapes. And he won't poop on your rug. Will you, Cinnamon? Go ahead, stand up and tell him you won't. Stand up, Cinnamon."

Cinnamon stood on my sneaker. His eyes shone like black pearls.

"Doesn't he have the cutest ears?"

Who notices a rat's ears? I looked. She was right. "Yeah," I said, "I guess he does."

"Tickle him behind his ears. He loves that."

I swallowed hard. I reached down with the tips of my

....

No comment I do not want to answer your question

getting a little carried away wrong, exaggerating

sleep-overs parties where people stay at each other's houses

Her voice was mock-pouty. She pretended to be upset.

two forefingers and tickled the tiny, furry spaces behind the rat's ears. I guessed he enjoyed it. He didn't move. And then, surprising myself, I moved one fingertip in front of his nose, and he licked me. It had never occurred to me that rats do that. His tongue was half the size of my little fingernail. I would have guessed it was rough, like a cat's, but it wasn't; it was smooth.

And then he was no longer on my foot—he was on my shoulder. I yelped. I tried to swat him off, but he dug into my shirt with his fingernails. Meanwhile, Stargirl was **cracking up**. I could see the shadow shaking.

"Let me guess," she said. "Cinnamon jumped onto your shoulder."

"You got it," I said.

"And you're thinking about how rats are supposed to go for people's throats."

"I wasn't," I said, "but now that you mention it . . . " I clamped my hands around my neck. I felt something in my ear. Whiskery. I yelped again. "He's eating my ear!"

Stargirl laughed some more. "He's **nuzzling** you. He likes you. Especially your ears. He never meets an ear he doesn't love. By the time he's done, that ear of yours will be **clean as a whistle**. Especially if there's some leftover peanut butter in it."

I could feel the tiny tongue **mopping the crevices** of my left ear. "It tickles!" I felt something else. "I feel teeth!"

"He's just scraping something off for you. You must have something crusty in there. Have you washed your ears lately?"

"None of your business."

....

cracking up laughing very hard
nuzzling getting close to; cuddling
clean as a whistle very clean
mopping the crevices cleaning the small parts

"Sorry. Didn't mean to get personal."

"I forgive you."

All was quiet for a while, except for the **snuffing** in my ear. I could hear the rat breathing. His tail drooped into my front shirt pocket.

"Do you want to confess now?"

"Confess what?" I said.

"That you're actually starting to like having a rodent poking around in your ear."

I smiled. I nodded, dislodging the rat's nose for a moment. "I confess."

More silence, tiny breathing in my ear.

"Well," she said at last, "we have to go in now. Say good night, Cinnamon."

No, I thought, *don't go.*

"I still have another ear," I said.

"If he does that one, he'll never want to leave you, and I'll be jealous. Come on, Cinnamon. Time **for beddy bye**."

Cinnamon went on snuffing.

"He's not coming, is he?"

"Nope."

"Then just take hold of him and put him on the ground."

I did so. As soon as I put the rat down, he scooted under the tailpipe and out of sight on the other side of the car.

The shadow **withdrew**. I heard the front door open. Light gushed out. "'Night, Leo."

"'Night," I called.

....

snuffing sounds
for beddy bye to go to sleep
withdrew disappeared

94

I didn't want to leave. I wished I could **curl up** right there on the driveway and go to sleep. I had been crouching for a long time. It was **a chore** just to stand. I was halfway home before I could walk right.

....

curl up get comfortable
a chore hard

17

Just two weeks before, I had found out she knew my name, and now I was **loopy with love**. I was floating. I floated up the white light that washed my sheets and slept on the moon. In school I was a yellow balloon, smiling and lazy, floating above the classrooms. I felt a faint tug on my string. Far below, Kevin was calling, "You're in love, dude!" I merely smiled and rolled over and drifted dreamily out a window.

This state lasted until lunch, when suddenly I became **self-conscious**. I was certain that everyone in school knew. They would be waiting for me, turning as I entered the lunchroom, staring. I was uncomfortable **in the spotlight**, always had been. I was happy to stay behind the camera and let Kevin take the bows out front.

So I hid for those thirty-five minutes in the gym equipment room. I sat atop a rolled-up wrestling mat, kicking a volleyball against the opposite wall. I had nothing to eat—I had intended to buy—but I wasn't hungry.

After school we found each other, not that we had to look.

She took Cinnamon from her bag and put him on her shoulder. "Shake paws with Leo, Cinnamon."

Cinnamon and I shook paws.

"Do you believe in **enchanted** places?" she said.

"You talking to me or the rat?"

She smiled. She dazzled. "You."

---

loopy with love acting silly because I was in love
self-conscious nervous, insecure
in the spotlight being the center of attention
enchanted magical

"I don't know," I said. "I never thought about it."

"I'm going to show you one."

"What if I don't want to see it?"

"You think you have a choice?"

She grabbed my hand and almost pulled me off my feet, laughing out loud, and we **flew** across the school fields, swinging hands for all the world to see.

We walked for miles, out past the business park, MicaTronics, the golf course, into the desert. "Look familiar?" she said.

By now, Cinnamon was riding my shoulder. And I was carrying the ukulele, strumming nonsense. "It's where we came that day," I said.

She gave a snort. "*We? I* was coming out here, *you* were half a mile behind." She poked my shoulder. "*Sneaking* after me." She poked me again, hard this time, but her eyes were twinkling. "*Stalking* me."

I acted horrified, hurt. "Stalking? I was not stalking. I was just lagging behind a little, that's all."

"Following me."

I shrugged. "So?"

"Why?"

I could feel a million reasons, but there were no words to express them. "I don't know."

"You liked me."

I smiled.

....

flew ran quickly

She gave a snort. She laughed.

Stalking Following, Hunting

"You were **smitten** with me. **You were speechless to behold my beauty.** You had never met anyone so fascinating. You thought of me every waking minute. You dreamed about me. You couldn't stand it. You couldn't let such wonderfulness out of your sight. You *had* to follow me."

I turned to Cinnamon. He licked my nose. "Don't give yourself so much credit. It was your rat I was after."

She laughed, and the desert sang.

To the person who expects every desert to be barren sand dunes, the Sonoran must come as a surprise. Not only are there no dunes, there's no sand. At least not the sort of sand you find at the beach. The ground does have a sandy color to it, or gray, but your feet won't sink in. It's hard, as if it's been **tamped**. And pebbly. And glinting with—what else—mica.

But you don't notice the ground much. What you notice are the saguaros. To the newcomer from the East, it's as simple as that. The desert seems to be a brown wasteland of dry, prickly scrub whose only purpose is to serve as a setting for the majestic saguaros. Then, little by little, the plants of the desert begin to identify themselves: the porcupiny yucca, the beaver tail and prickly pear and barrel cacti, buckhorn and staghorn and devil's fingers, the tall, sky-reaching tendrils of the ocotillo.

We walked a weaving line around the plant life, up and down washes and gullies, the Maricopas looming lavender in the distance.

....

smitten in love

You were speechless to behold my beauty. You thought I was so pretty that you could not speak.

tamped pressed down

"When you turned and ran that day," she said, "I called after you."

"You did?"

"I whispered."

"Whispered? How'd you expect me to hear?"

"I don't know," she said. "I just thought you would."

I strummed the uke. **I squared my shoulders.** Giving a rat a ride **improves the posture.**

"You're shy, aren't you?" she said.

"What makes you think that?"

She laughed. "Were you embarrassed when I pulled you along after school today? All those kids looking?"

"Nah."

"Are you lying?"

"Yeah."

She laughed. I seemed to be good at making her laugh.

I glanced back. The highway was out of sight. **"Do you have the time?"** I said.

"Nobody has the time," she said. "The time cannot be owned." She threw out her arms and twirled till her multicolored skirt looked like a pinwheel taffy. "The time is free to everyone!"

"Sorry I asked," I said.

She hung her sunflower bag on a cactus arm and cartwheeled toward the Maricopas. Crazily, I felt like joining her. I told myself I couldn't because I was loaded down with a

....

I squared my shoulders. I walked proudly.

improves the posture makes you stand straight

"Nah." "No."

Do you have the time? Do you know what time it is?

ukulele and a rat. I picked up her bag and followed.

When she decided to walk like a normal human again, I told her she was goofy.

She stopped, turned to me, and bowed grandly. "Thank you, good sir."

Then she took my arm as if we were strolling down a promenade and she said, "Scream, Leo."

"Huh?"

"Just throw your head back and let it all out. **Scream your ears off.** Nobody will hear you."

"Why would I want to do that?"

She turned her astonished eyes on me. "Why wouldn't you?"

I pointed to Cinnamon. "If he screams first, then I will." And I changed the subject. "Are we ever going to get to this enchanted place?" I felt silly just saying the words.

"Just a little farther," she said.

I humored her. "So how do you know an enchanted place when you come to it?"

"You'll see," she said. She squeezed my hand. "Did you know there's a country with officially designated 'enchanted places'?"

"No," I said. "Where would that be? Oz?"

"Iceland."

"Imagine that."

"I'm ignoring your **sarcasm.** I think it would be neat if we had that here. You'd be walking or riding along, and there

....

Scream your ears off. Scream as loud as you can.

humored her played along with her

sarcasm doubtful attitude

would be this stone marker with a brass plate: 'Enchanted Site. U.S. Department of Interior.'"

"We'd **litter it up**," I said.

She stared at me, her smile gone. "Would we?"

I felt bad, as if I had ruined something. "Not really," I told her. "Not if there's a Don't Be a Litterbug sign."

A minute later she stopped. "We're here."

I looked around. The place couldn't have been more ordinary. The only notable presence was a tall, **dilapidated** saguaro, a bundle of sticks, in worse shape than Archie's Señor. The rest was gray scrub and tumbleweed and a few prickly pears. "I thought it might look different," I said.

"Special? Scenic?"

"Yeah, I guess."

"It's a different kind of scenery," she said. "Shoes off."

We pulled off our shoes.

"Sit."

We sat, legs crossed. Cinnamon scampered down my arm and onto the ground.

Stargirl shrieked, "Stop!" She scooped up the rat and put him in her bag. "Owls, hawks, snakes. He'd be a tasty meal."

"So," I said, "when does the enchantment start?"

We were sitting side by side, facing the mountains.

"It started when the earth was born." Her eyes were closed. Her face was **golden** in the setting sun. "It never stops. It is, always. It's just here."

"So what do we do?"

....

litter it up ruin it by making it dirty
dilapidated bad looking; dying
golden glowing, shining

She smiled. "That's the secret." Her cupped hands rested in her lap. "We do nothing. Or as close to nothing as we can." Her face turned slowly to me, though her eyes remained closed. "Have you ever done nothing?"

I laughed. "My mother thinks I do it all the time."

"Don't tell her I said so, but your mother is wrong." She turned back to the sun. "It's really hard to do nothing totally. Even just sitting here, like this, **our bodies are churning, our minds are chattering**. There's a **whole commotion** going on inside us."

"That's bad?" I said.

"It's bad if we want to know what's going on outside ourselves."

"Don't we have eyes and ears for that?"

She nodded. "They're okay most of the time. But sometimes they just get in the way. The earth is speaking to us, but we can't hear because of all the racket our senses are making. Sometimes we need to erase them, erase our senses. Then— maybe—the earth will touch us. **The universe will speak. The stars will whisper.**"

The sun was glowing orange now, clipping the mountains' purple crests.

"So how do I become this nothing?"

"I'm not sure," she said. "There's no one answer to that. You have to find your own way. Sometimes I try to erase myself. I imagine a big pink soft soap eraser, and it's going back and forth, back and forth, and it starts down at my toes, back and

....

our bodies are churning, our minds are chattering we feel things in our bodies, we are always thinking

whole commotion lot of thoughts and processes

The universe will speak. The stars will whisper. We will feel more than just what our five senses, or bodies, tell us.

forth, back and forth, and there they go—poof!—my toes are gone. And then my feet. And then my ankles. But that's the easy part. The hard part is erasing my senses—my eyes, my ears, my nose, my tongue. And last to go is my brain. My thoughts, memories, all the voices inside my head. That's the hardest, erasing my thoughts." She chuckled faintly. "My pumpkin. And then, if I've done a good job, I'm erased. I'm gone. I'm nothing. And then the world is free to flow into me like water into an empty bowl."

"And?" I said.

"And . . . I see. I hear. But not with eyes and ears. I'm not outside my world anymore, and I'm not really inside it either. The thing is, there's no difference anymore between me and the universe. The boundary is gone. I am it and it is me. I am a stone, a cactus thorn. I am rain." She smiled dreamily. "I like that most of all, being rain."

"Am I the first one you've brought out here?"

She didn't answer. She faced the mountains, **bathed in sun syrup,** her face as still and peaceful as I've ever seen a face.

"Stargirl—"

"Shhhh."

That was the last sound either of us made for a long time. We sat side by side, **lotus style,** facing west. I closed my eyes. I tried to be perfectly still—and promptly found out that she was right. I could immobilize my arms and legs, but **inside me it was rush hour in downtown Phoenix.** I had never been so aware of my breath and my heartbeat, not to mention

....

bathed in sun syrup looking golden in the sun

lotus style cross-legged

inside me it was rush hour in downtown Phoenix I could not calm down other assorted grumblings and gurglings. And my head—it just wouldn't close down. Every question, every stray thought from miles around came wandering into my brain, sniffing about, scratching at my attention.

But I tried. I tried the eraser, but it wouldn't even wipe out the first toe. I tried to imagine I was sawdust blowing away with the wind. Swallowed by a whale. Dissolving away like Alka-Seltzer. Nothing worked. I could not make myself disappear.

I peeked. I knew I wasn't supposed to, but I did. Clearly, she had erased herself. She was gone. She was **serenity**. Her lips faintly smiling. Her golden skin. The glowing thread-ends of her hair. She seemed to have been dipped in sunlight and set here to dry. I felt a **pang of jealousy**, that she could be sitting next to me and not know it. That she could be somewhere most wonderful and I could not be there, too.

Then I saw the rat. He had crawled out of the bag. He was sitting on it much as we were, his front paws—I kept thinking of them as tiny hands, they were so human-like—dangling before him. He, too, was not moving. He, too, was facing the sunset, his **pelt** the color of a new penny. His peppercorn eyes were fully open.

I knew it must have been a trick she had taught him, or imitative rodent behavior. Still, I couldn't help thinking there was more to it, that the whiskered little fellow was having an experience of his own—which might include **digestion in a critter's stomach** if Stargirl's fears came true. As quietly as

....

serenity peaceful, quiet
pang of jealousy little jealous
pelt fur
digestion in a critter's stomach being eaten

possible, I reached over and scooped him up. I held him in both hands. He did not struggle or squirm, but resumed facing the sunset with his tiny chin resting on my forefinger. In my fingertips I could feel his heartbeat. I drew him closer to my chest. **I dared any varmint to come near.**

I took a deep breath and closed my eyes for another try at enchantment. I don't think I succeeded. I think Cinnamon was a better eraser than I. I tried. I tried so hard I almost squeaked, but I could not seem to leave myself, and the cosmos did not visit me. I could not stop wondering what time it was.

But something did happen. A small thing. I was aware of stepping over a line, of taking one step into territory new to me. It was a territory of peace, of silence. I had never experienced such utter silence before, such stillness. The commotion within me went on, but at a lower volume, as if someone had turned down my dial. And an **eerie** thing happened. While I never did totally lose awareness of myself, I believe I did, **so to speak,** lose Cinnamon. I no longer felt his pulse, his presence, in my hands. It seemed we were no longer separate, but were one.

When the sun fell behind the mountains, I felt it as a faint coolness on my face.

I don't know how long my eyes were closed. When I opened them, she was gone. Alarmed, I jerked around. She was standing **off a ways,** smiling. Evening had come. While my eyes were

....

I dared any varmint to come near. I would protect him.
eerie strange, scary
so to speak sort of; kind of
off a ways away from me

closed, the **mountains' dusky lavender had drifted** over the desert.

We put on our shoes. We **headed for** the highway. I expected her to interrogate me, but she did not. One moment the moon was not there, and then it was, then one bright star. We walked across the desert **hand in hand**, saying nothing.

....

mountains' dusky lavender had drifted sun going behind the mountains made shadows

headed for walked toward

hand in hand holding hands

BEFORE YOU MOVE ON...

1. **Metaphor** Reread page 96. Why does Leo say: "I was a yellow balloon"?

2. **Conclusions** Why does Stargirl take Leo to her enchanted place? What does she want to teach Leo?

LOOK AHEAD Read pages 107–123 to learn about the "shunning."

18

We were alone. We were the only ones in school.

At least that's how it seemed in the following days.

As I went about my day, I felt her going about hers. I sensed her movement, her presence in distant parts of the building. Walking the halls between classes, I didn't have to see her, I knew she was there: unseen in the mob heading my way, about to turn a corner five classroom doors down. **I homed in on the beacon** of her smile. As we approached each other, the noise and the students around us **melted away** and we were utterly alone, passing, smiling, holding each other's eyes, floors and walls gone, two people in a universe of space and stars.

And then one day I began to discover that we were more alone than I had dreamed.

It was a Thursday. Normally on that day, after third period, Stargirl and I would pass each other on the second floor around the teachers' lounge. We would smile and say hi and continue on our way to our separate classes. On this day, impulsively, I fell in alongside her.

"How about an escort?" I said.

She grinned slyly. "Anybody in mind?"

We touched little fingers and walked on. Her next class was on the first floor, so we went down the nearest stairway. We were walking side by side. That's when I noticed.

No one spoke to us.

I homed in on the beacon I focused on the brightness
melted away seemed to disappear
How about an escort? Would you like someone to walk with?

No one nodded to us.

No one smiled at us.

No one looked at us.

A crowded stairway, and no shoulder, no sleeve brushed us.

Students climbing the steps veered to the railing or wall. Except for Stargirl jabbering in my ear, the usual raucous chatter was absent.

Mostly what I noticed were the eyes. Faces turned up from the steps below, but the eyes never connected with us. They went right on through us as if **they were gamma rays**. Or they **nipped our ears and rattled off among the walls and other eyes**. I had an urge to look down at myself, to make sure I was there.

At lunch I said to Kevin, "Nobody looks at me."

He was staring at his sandwich.

"Kevin!" I snapped. "Now *you're* doing it."

He came up laughing. He looked **me square in the** eyes. "Sorry."

Usually there were others at the table. Today there was only us. I leaned across my lunch. "Kevin, what's going on?"

He looked off, then back to me. "I was wondering when you'd notice. Kinda hoping you wouldn't."

"Notice *what*?"

He stalled by taking a bite of tuna salad sandwich. He took his time chewing. He drank orangeade from a straw. "First of all, it's not you."

I pulled back. I held out my hands. "It's not me. What's that

....

they were gamma rays we were not there

nipped our ears and rattled off among the walls and other eyes glanced at us but then looked away at something else

me square in the directly into my

supposed to mean?"

"It's who you're with."

I sat there, blinking, staring at him. "Stargirl?"

He nodded.

"Okay," I said. "So?"

He stared at me some more, chewed, swallowed, sipped, looked away, looked back. "They're not talking to her."

The words didn't stick. "What do you mean? Who's 'they'?"

He cocked his head at the sea of tables and eaters. "Them."

"Who them?" I said, too **unhinged** to laugh at my grammar.

He wet his lips. "All of them." He shrugged. "Well, almost." His eyes drifted over my shoulder. "There're still two girls sitting with her."

I glanced back. At the height of Stargirl's popularity, kids had been pulling chairs from other tables to squeeze around hers. Now it was just Stargirl, Dori Dilson, and a ninth-grader.

"So," I said, "exactly what is going on?"

He sipped from his straw. "**The silent treatment is going on.** Nobody's talking to her."

It still wasn't sticking. "What do you mean, 'nobody's talking to her'? What, did everybody have a meeting in the gym and vote on it?"

"It wasn't that official. It just happened. **Got up steam.**"

I gaped at him. "When? When did it start? How? Why?" I was beginning to screech.

"I don't know exactly. After the basketball stuff, I guess.

....

unhinged upset, confused

The silent treatment is going on. Everyone has decided not to talk to her.

Got up steam. Then everyone decided to do it.

That really **ticked off** a lot of people."

"The basketball stuff."

He nodded.

"The basketball stuff," I repeated dumbly.

He put down his sandwich. "Leo, don't act like you don't know what I'm talking about. Cheering for the other team? What did you think, people thought that was *cute?*"

"It was her, Kevin. It was harmless. Weird maybe, but harmless. It was *her.*"

He nodded slowly. "Yeah, well, I guess that's what I'm saying. It's not just one thing she did. It's everything. Don't tell me you never noticed. Remember a certain tomato?"

"Kevin, a couple of months ago everybody stood and cheered in the auditorium when she won the oratorical contest."

"Hey"—he gestured defensively —"tell *them.*"

"One person threw the tomato. One."

Kevin snickered. "Yeah, and a thousand wanted to. Did you notice the cheers when it happened? People blame her. For the team losing. **For our undefeated season going down the toilet.**"

I wasn't sure Kevin was still talking about "them."

"Kevin—" I felt myself **pleading**. "She was only a *cheerleader.*"

"Leo"—he was pointing—"you asked me what was going on, I told you." He stood up and took his tray to the belt.

I stared at his empty chair until he returned.

"Kevin . . . the Happy Birthday songs, the Valentine cards,

----

ticked off angered

For our undefeated season going down the toilet. For making us stop winning all the games.

pleading begging him to listen; arguing

all the nice things she does for people . . . doesn't that count for something?"

The bell rang.

He got up. He gathered his books. He shrugged. "I guess not."

For the rest of the day, and the next and the next, I grew increasingly **paranoid**. Walking with her in and around the school, I was intensely aware that the nature of our aloneness had changed. It was no longer a cozy, tunnel-of-love sweetness, but a chilling **isolation**. We never had to veer, never had to make way for someone else; everyone made way for us. Hallway crowds fell away from us. Except for Hillari Kimble. Whenever we passed her, she tilted toward us with a gloating smirk on her face.

As for Stargirl, she didn't seem to notice. She jabbered constantly in my ear. While I smiled and nodded to her, **frost formed on the back of my neck.**

....

paranoid nervous, anxious

isolation loneliness

frost formed on the back of my neck I felt like I was starting to not like Stargirl, either

19

"The Amish in Pennsylvania have a word for it."

"What's that?" I said.

"Shunning."

I was at Archie's. I had to talk to someone.

"Well, that's what's happening."

"The shunnee, so to speak, has gotten himself in **dutch** with the church, so he's **excommunicated**. The whole community is in on it. Unless he **repents**, nobody speaks to him for the rest of his life. Not even his family."

"What?!"

"That's right. Not even his family."

"What about his wife?"

"Wife. Kids. Everybody." His pipe had gone out. He relit it with a stick match. "I believe the idea is to drive him away. But some stay, continue working the farm, having dinner. If he passes the salt to his wife, she ignores it. If the bishop had his way, the pigs and chickens would ignore him. It's as if he doesn't exist."

I nodded. "I know the feeling."

We were on the back porch. I stared out at Señor Saguaro.

He said, "Does it happen to you when you're not with her?"

"No," I said. "At least I don't think so. But when I'm with her, I feel like it's aimed at me, too."

A small pipe cloud left the corner of his mouth. He smiled

"Shunning." "Ignoring."

dutch big trouble

excommunicated been forced to leave

repents asks for forgiveness

sadly. **"Poor dolphin. Caught in a tuna net."**

I picked up Barney, the Paleocene rodent skull. I wondered if someone would be holding Cinnamon's head 60 million years from now. "So, what should I do?"

Archie waved his hand. "Oh, well, that's the easy part. Stay away from her: your problem's *kaput*."

I sneered. "Great advice. You know it's not that easy."

He did know, of course, but he wanted me to say it. I told him about the valentine, the night in her driveway, the walk in the desert. The question that came to mind then sounded silly, but it persisted: "Do you believe in enchanted places?"

He took the pipe from his mouth and looked straight at me. "Absolutely."

I was confused. "But you're a scientist. A man of science."

"A man of bones. You can't be **up to your eyeballs in** bones and not believe in enchanted places."

I looked at Barney. I ran my fingertip along the hard line of his two-inch jaw, rough like a cat's tongue. Sixty million years in my hands. I looked at Archie. "Why can't she be . . . "

He finished for me: " . . . like everybody else?"

He stood up and stepped down from the porch onto the desert—for his back yard, except for the shed where he kept his digging tools, *was* the desert. Nature did the landscaping. I put down Barney and joined him. We ambled toward Señor Saguaro.

"Not like everybody else," I said. "Not exactly. Not totally. But . . . Archie . . . " I stopped. He stopped. I turned full-face to

....

"Poor dolphin. Caught in a tuna net." "You are somewhere you do not belong."

kaput over, gone

up to your eyeballs in surrounded by

him. My thoughts and feelings were a wild, conflicting jumble. After staring stupidly at him for a long time, I blurted, "She cheers for the other team!"

Archie pulled the pipe from his mouth, as if to better **digest my words**. He raised one finger in the air. He nodded **solemnly**. "Ahh, yes."

We resumed walking.

We walked on past the toolshed, past Señor Saguaro. Occasionally I picked up a stone and flung it toward the purple Maricopas.

Archie said, almost in a whisper, "She's not easy to **put into words**, is she?"

I shook my head.

"An unusual girl," he said. "Could see that from the first. And her parents, as ordinary, in a nice way, as could be. How did this girl come to be? I used to ask myself. Sometimes I thought she should be teaching me. She seems to **be in touch with** something that the rest of us are missing." He looked at me. "Hm?"

I nodded.

He turned the mahogany bowl of his pipe upside down and rapped it with his knuckle. A small stream of ash spilled onto a thicket of dead mesquite.

He pointed the pipe stem at me. "You know, there's a place we all inhabit, but we don't much think about it, we're scarcely conscious of it, and it lasts for less than a minute a day."

"What's that?" I said.

....

digest my words understand me
solemnly seriously
put into words describe; talk about
be in touch with have, understand

"It's in the morning, for most of us. It's that time, those few seconds when we're coming out of sleep but we're not really awake yet. For those few seconds we're something more primitive than what we are about to become. We have just slept the sleep of our most distant ancestors, and something of them and their world still clings to us. For those few moments we are unformed, uncivilized. We are not the people we know as ourselves, but creatures more in tune with a tree than a keyboard. We are untitled, unnamed, natural, suspended between was and will be, the tadpole before the frog, the worm before the butterfly. We are, for a few brief moments, anything and everything we could be. And then . . . "

He pulled out his pouch and repacked his pipe. Cherryscent flew. He struck a match. The pipe bowl, like some predator, or seducer, drew down the flame. " . . . and then—ah—we open our eyes and the day is before us, and"—he snapped his fingers—"we become ourselves."

Like so many of Archie's words, **they seemed not to enter through my ears but to settle on my skin, there to burrow like tiny eggs awaiting the rain of my maturity, when they would hatch and I at last would understand.**

We walked in silence. Yellow blooms had appeared on a cactus, and for some reason that made me incredibly sad. The purple of the mountains flowed like watercolor.

"They *hate* her," I said.

He stopped. He looked intently at me. He turned me around and we headed back. He put his arm around my

----

they seemed not to enter through ears but to settle on my
skin, there to burrow like tiny eggs awaiting the rain of
my maturity, when they would hatch and I at last would
understand I felt I would understand them when I got older

shoulder. "Let's consult Señor Saguaro."

Shortly we were standing **before the derelict giant**. I never understood how the Señor managed to convey a sense of dignity, majesty even, considering his stick-rickety, see-through skeleton and the ridiculous, leathery crumple of hide about his foot, his fallen britches. Archie always spoke to him with respectful formality, as to a judge or visiting **dignitary**.

"Good day, Señor Saguaro," he began. "I believe you know my friend and charter member of the Loyal Order of the Stone Bone, Mr. Borlock." He whispered an aside to me: "I'm a little rusty, but I think I'll use Spanish now. He prefers it on delicate matters." He turned back to the cactus. *"Parece, Señor Borlock aquí es la víctima de un 'shunning' de sus compañeros estudiantes en el liceo. El objeto principal del 'shunning' es la enamorada del Señor Borlock, nuestra propia Señorita Niña Estrella. El está en búsqueda de preguntas."*

As Archie spoke, he looked up toward the elf owl hole. Now he turned back to me and whispered, "I asked for questions."

"Questions?" I whispered. "What about answers?"

But he was turning from me, tilting his head toward the great cactus, his finger on his lips—"Shh"—his eyes closed.

I waited.

At last he nodded and turned back to me. "The esteemed Señor says there is only one question."

"What's that?" I said.

"He says **it all boils down to this**—if I'm translating correctly: Whose **affection** do you value more, hers or the

....

before the derelict giant in front of the dying cactus

dignitary important person

it all boils down to this this is what matters the most

affection love, caring

others'? The Señor says everything will **follow from that**."

I wasn't sure I understood the Señor any more than I understood Archie half the time, but I said nothing, and I went home. In bed that night, as the moonlight **reached high tide under my chin**, I realized that in fact I understood the question perfectly. I just didn't want to answer it.

....

follow from that change when you answer that question

reached high tide under my chin came through my window

20

Twice a week the results of the state basketball tournament were posted on the plywood roadrunner in the courtyard. The surviving teams were into the sectionals now; then would come the regionals; then, with only two teams left, the big show, the Arizona state championship. Glendale, the team we had lost to, got **bitter, masochistic** attention on the roadrunner with scores in foot-high numerals, as they continued to win and move through the tournament.

Meanwhile, Stargirl was involved in a tournament of her own, the oratorical contest. As Mica High's winner, she qualified for the district "talk-off," as the *Times* called it. It took place in the auditorium of Red Rock High School, and **lo and behold**, Stargirl won that, too. Next stop was the state finals in Phoenix on the third Friday in April.

In my homeroom, when the announcement came over the PA about Stargirl winning the district title, I was about to let out a cheer, but I caught myself. Several people booed.

Getting ready for the finals, Stargirl practiced on me. Most often we went into the desert. She did not use notes, nor did her words seem memorized. Each time she gave the speech, it was different. She seemed to insert new material as **it popped into her head**. She matched her words so perfectly that the speech was not a speech at all, but one creature's voice in the wild, as natural as a raven's caw or a coyote's howl at midnight.

---

bitter, masochistic mean, angry
lo and behold of course
it popped into her head she thought of it

I sat cross-legged on the ground, Cinnamon sat on me. We listened **in rapture**, and so, I half believed, did the tumbleweed and cacti, the desert, the mountains, all listening to the girl in the longfalling skirt. What a shame, I thought, to pack her performance into a schedule and present it to rows of plush-back seats in an auditorium. Once, incredibly, an elf owl landed atop a saguaro not ten feet from where she was speaking. It paused for a full minute before ducking into its hole.

Of course, we did other things, too. We walked. We talked. We rode bikes. Though I had my driver's license, I bought a cheap **secondhand** bicycle so I could ride with her. Sometimes she led the way, sometimes I did. Whenever we could, we rode side by side.

She was bendable light: she shone around every corner of my day.

She taught me to **revel**. She taught me to wonder. She taught me to laugh. My sense of humor had always measured up to everyone else's; but timid, **introverted** me, I showed it sparingly: I was a smiler. In her presence I threw back my head and laughed out loud for the first time in my life.

She saw things. I had not known there was so much to see.
She was forever tugging my arm and saying, "Look!"
I would look around, seeing nothing. "Where?"
She would point. "There."
In the beginning I still could not see. She might be pointing to a doorway, or a person, or the sky. But such things were so common to my eyes, so undistinguished, that they would

....

in rapture intensely, eagerly
secondhand used
revel celebrate
introverted shy

register as "nothing." **I walked in a gray world of nothings.**

So she would stop and point out that the front door of the house we were passing was blue. And that the last time we had passed it, it had been green. And that as near as she could tell, someone who lived in that house painted the front door a different color several times a year.

Or she would whisper to me that the old man sitting alone on the bench at the Tudor Village shopping center was holding his hearing aid in his hand, and he was smiling, and he wore a coat and tie as if he were going somewhere special, and pinned onto his lapel was a tiny American flag.

Or she would kneel down and pull me down with her and show me the ants, two of them, lugging the lopped leg of a beetle twenty times their size across the sidewalk, as might two men, were they strong as ants, carry a full-grown tree from one end of town to the other.

After a while I began to see better. When she said "Look!" and I followed her pointing finger, I saw. Eventually it became a contest: who would see first? When I finally did it—said "Look!" and pointed and tugged *her* sleeve—I was as proud as a first-grader with a star on his paper.

And there was more to her seeing than that. What she saw, she felt. **Her eyes went straight to her heart.** The old man on the bench, for example, made her cry. The lumberjack ants made her laugh. The door of many colors put her in such a **snit** of curiosity that I had to drag her away; she felt she could not proceed with her life until she knocked on such a door.

....

I walked in a gray world of nothings. I did not pay attention to the little things in life.

Her eyes went straight to her heart. She was affected emotionally by what she saw.

snit state, moment

120

She told me how she would run the *Mica Times* if she were the editor. Crime would be on page 10, ants and old men and painted doors on page 1. She made up headlines:

ANTS HAUL MONSTER LOAD
ACROSS VAST, BARREN WALK

MYSTERY SMILE: OLD MAN
NODS OFF AT TUDOR VILLAGE

DOOR BEGS: KNOCK ME!

I told her I wanted to be a TV director. She said she wanted to **be a silver-lunch-truck driver.**

"Huh?" I said.

"You know," she said, "people work all morning and then it's twelve o'clock. The secretaries in the offices walk out the door, the construction workers put down their hard hats and hammers, and everybody's hungry, and they look up and there I am! No matter where they are, no matter where they work, I'm there. I have a whole fleet of silver lunch trucks. They go everywhere. 'Let Lunch Come to You!' That's my slogan. Just seeing my silver lunch truck makes them happy." She described how she would roll up the side panels and everyone would practically faint at the cloud of wonderful smells. Hot food, cold food, Chinese, Italian, you name it. Even a salad bar. "They can't believe how much food I fit into my truck. No matter

....

be a silver-lunch-truck driver drive a silver truck that would sell lunches where you are—out in the desert, the mountains, even down in the mines—if you want my silver lunch service, I get it to you. I find a way."

I **tagged along** on missions. One day she bought a small plant, an African violet in a plastic pot on sale for ninety-nine cents at a drugstore.

"Who's it for?" I asked her.

"I'm not exactly sure," she said. "I just know that someone at an address on Marion Drive is in the hospital for surgery, so I thought whoever's back home could use a little cheering up."

"How do you know this stuff?" I said.

She gave me a mischievous grin. "I have my ways."

We went to the house on Marion Drive. She reached into the **saddle pack** behind her bicycle seat. She pulled out a handful of ribbons. She chose a pale violet one that matched the color of the tiny blossoms and stuffed the remaining ribbons back into the seat pack. She tied the violet ribbon around the pot. I held her bike while she set the plant by the front door.

Riding away, I said, "Why don't you leave a card or something with your name on it?"

The question surprised her. "Why should I?"

Her question surprised me. "Well, I don't know, it's just the way people do things. They expect it. They get a gift, they expect to know where it came from."

"Is that important?"

"Yeah, I guess—"

....

tagged along went with her
saddle pack storage bag

I never **finished that thought**. My tires **shuddered** as I slammed my bike to a halt. She stopped ahead of me. She backed up. She stared.

"Leo, what is it?"

I wagged my head. I grinned. I pointed to her. "It was *you*."

"Me what?"

"Two years ago. My birthday. I found a package on my front step. A porcupine necktie. I never found out who gave it to me."

She walked her bike alongside mine. She grinned. "A mystery."

"Where did you find it?" I said.

"I didn't. I had my mother make it."

She didn't seem to want to **dwell on the subject**. She started pedaling and we continued on our way.

"Where were we?" she said.

"Getting credit," I said.

"What about it?"

"Well, it's nice to get credit."

The spokes of her rear wheel spun behind the curtain of her long skirt. She looked like a photograph from a hundred years ago. She turned her wide eyes on me. "Is it?" she said.

....

finished that thought completed what I wanted to say

shuddered shook

dwell on the subject keep talking about it

BEFORE YOU MOVE ON...

1. **Character** Leo is upset by the "shunning," but Stargirl does not seem to care. What does this show about Leo?

2. **Inference** Leo thinks Stargirl gave him the necktie. Why?

LOOK AHEAD Read to page 137 to learn what Stargirl loves to do.

21

On weekends and after dinner, we delivered many potted violets. And CONGRATULATIONS! balloons. And cards **of many sentiments**. She made her own cards. She wasn't a great artist. Her people were stick figures. The girls all had triangle skirts and pigtails. You would never mistake one of her cards for a Hallmark, but I have never seen cards more heartfelt. They were meaningful in the way that a schoolchild's homemade Christmas card is meaningful. She never left her name.

But finally, after much pestering from me, she did tell me how she knew what was going on in people's lives. It was simple, she said. She read the daily paper. Not the headlines or the front page or the sports page or the comics or the TV listings or the Hollywood gossip. What she read were the parts that most people ignored, the parts without headlines and pictures, the **boondocks of the paper**: the hospital admissions, the death notices, the birthday and wedding announcements, the police **blotter**, the coming events calendar.

Most of all, she read the fillers.

"I *love* fillers!" she exclaimed.

"What are fillers?" I said.

She explained that fillers are little items that are not considered important enough to be a story or to have a headline. They're never more than one column wide, never more than an inch or two deep. They are most commonly

---

of many sentiments about many different things
boondocks of the paper parts no one paid attention to
blotter records

found at the bottoms of inside pages, where **the eye seldom travels.** If the editors had their way, they would never use fillers. But sometimes a reporter doesn't write quite enough words, and the story doesn't reach all the way to the bottom of the page. The paper can't have a blank space there, so the editor dumps in a filler. A filler doesn't need to be "news." It doesn't need to be important. It doesn't even need to be read. All it's asked to do is take up space.

A filler might come from anywhere and be about anything. It might tell how many pounds of rice a typical Chinese person eats in a lifetime. Or say something about beetles in Sumatra. Or the filler might come from down the street. It might mention that so-and-so's cat is missing. Or that so-and-so has a collection of antique marbles.

"I search through fillers like a prospector digging for gold," she said.

"So that's it?" I said. "You read the papers?"

"No," she said, "that's not all. There's also the place where I get my hair cut. I always overhear good stuff there. And of course there're bulletin boards. Do you know how many bulletin boards there are in town?"

"Sure," I said **facetiously**, "I count them every day."

"So do I," she said, not kidding. "So far, I'm up to forty-one."

Offhand, I couldn't think of one, except the plywood roadrunner. "What do you learn from bulletin boards?"

"Oh . . . somebody just opened a business. Somebody lost a

---

the eye seldom travels a reader hardly ever looks
facetiously jokingly
Offhand Without thinking about it for a while; Right then

dog. Somebody needs a companion."

"Who advertises for a companion?" I said. "Who needs one that bad?"

"Lonely people," she said. "Old people. Just somebody to sit with them for a while."

I pictured Stargirl sitting in a dark room with an old woman. I couldn't picture myself doing the same thing. Sometimes she seemed so **far** from me.

We were passing Pisa Pizza. "There's a bulletin board in there," she said.

It was just inside the door. It was smothered with business cards and notices. I pointed to one that said "Odd Jobs—Ask for Mike," call this number. "So what's that tell you?" I said, with more challenge in my voice than I intended.

She read it. "Well, it could be that Mike lost his regular job and can't find another, so he's hiring himself out. Or even if he has a regular job, it's not enough to **make ends meet**. He's either not very neat, or he can't afford a whole piece of paper. This is just a **scrap**."

"So what would you do for him?" I said.

"Oh, I don't know. My parents might have an odd job they need done. Or maybe I do. Or maybe I could just send him a card."

"What kind of card would he get?"

"A **Keep-your-chin-up** card." She poked me. "Hey, want to play a card game?"

....

far different
make ends meet pay his bills
scrap small piece
Keep-your-chin-up Feel-better

I had a feeling she wasn't talking about poker. "Sure," I said.

She said she invented it. "All you need is your eyes and one other person. I pick somebody on the street, the mall, a store, wherever, and I follow them. Say it's a her. I follow her for fifteen minutes, not a minute more. I time myself. The game is, after fifteen minutes of watching her, I have to guess what kind of card she needs."

"But how can you get it to her?" I said. "You don't know where she lives."

"True. That's as far as it goes. That's why it's just a game. It's just for fun." She snuggled into me. She whispered in my ear, "Let's play."

I said sure.

She said we needed a mall. I usually steered us away from the Mica Mall—too many **silent-treatment MAHS kids hanging around there**. We drove ten miles to the Redstone Mall. It was a Saturday afternoon.

We picked out a woman. Lime-green **skort**. White sandals. We guessed her age was early forties. She was buying a soft pretzel—regular, salted—at Auntie Anne's. She carried the pretzel in a little white paper bag. We followed her into Suncoast Video. We overheard her ask for *When Harry Met Sally*. They didn't have it. She passed Sonoma, then came back and went in. She wandered about, touching pottery with one fingertip, feeling surfaces. She stopped before the dinner plates. She lifted one with a French café painted on it. "Van Gogh," Stargirl whispered. The lady seemed to think about the plate,

---

silent-treatment MAHS kids hanging around there
classmates were there who were not talking to us

skort skirt with shorts attached

even closed her eyes, holding it to her chest with both hands, as if **feeling vibrations**. But then she put it back and walked out. On to Sears. Lingerie. Bedclothes. I was uneasy, spying from behind a rack of frilly somethings. She was flipping through nightshirts when time ran out.

Stargirl and I **conferred** in the corridor.

"Okay," she said, "what do you think?"

"I think I feel like a stalker," I said.

"A good stalker," she said.

"You first," I said.

"Well, she's divorced and lonely. No wedding ring. Wants somebody in her life. A home life. She wishes she were Sally and her Harry would come along. She would make him dinner and snuggle with him at night. She tries to eat low-fat foods. She works for a travel agency. She took a free cruise last year, but all she met on the boat were **creeps**. Her name is Clarissa, she played the clarinet in high school, and her favorite soap is Irish Spring."

I boggled. "How do you know all that?"

She laughed. "I don't. I'm guessing. That's what makes it fun."

"So what card would you send her?"

She put her finger to her lips. "Hmm . . . to Clarissa I would send a While-you're-waiting-for-Harry-be-good-to-yourself card. How about you?"

"I would send a"—I **mulled over the phrasing**— "a Don't-let-Harry-catch-you-flicking card."

....

feeling vibrations the plate were shaking

conferred talked

creeps bad men

mulled over the phrasing thought how to say it

Now it was her turn to boggle. "Huh?"

"Didn't you see her **pick her nose**?" I said. "In Suncoast?"

"Not really. I saw her hand go to her nose, like she was scratching it or something."

"Yeah, or something. She was picking, that's what. She was quick and sneaky. A real **pro**."

She gave me a playful shove. "You're kidding."

I held up my hands. "I'm serious. She was standing in front of the comedies. Her finger went in and when it came out there was something on it. She carried it around for about a minute. And then, just as she was leaving Suncoast, when she thought nobody was looking, she flicked. I didn't see where it landed." She stared at me. I raised my right hand and put my left over my heart. "No lie."

She broke out laughing, so loudly I was embarrassed. She grabbed my arm with both hands to keep from collapsing. **Mallwalkers** stared.

We carded two others that day: a woman who spent her whole fifteen minutes feeling leather jackets—we called her Betty—and a man we called Adam because of his huge Adam's apple, which we renamed Adam's pumpkin. No more pick-'n'-flickers.

And I did have fun. Whether it came from the game or simply from being with her, I don't know. I do know I was surprised at how close I felt to Clarissa and Betty and Adam after watching them for only fifteen minutes.

Throughout the day, Stargirl had been dropping money.

....

pick her nose clean her nose with her finger
pro professional
Mallwalkers People who were walking in the mall

She was **the Johnny Appleseed of loose change**: a penny here, a nickel there. Tossed to the sidewalk, laid on a shelf or bench. Even quarters.

"I hate change," she said. "It's so . . . **jangly.**"

"Do you realize how much you must throw away in a year?" I said.

"Did you ever see a little kid's face when he spots a penny on a sidewalk?" she said.

When her change purse was empty, we drove back to Mica. Along the way she invited me to dinner at her house.

....

the Johnny Appleseed of loose change a person who drops extra coins for others to find

jangly noisy

22

Archie had claimed the Caraways were normal folks, but I still couldn't imagine Stargirl coming from an ordinary home. I think I expected **a leftover hippie scene from the 1960s.** Make love, not war. Her mother in a long skirt with a flower in her hair. Her father's face framed in muttonchop sideburns, saying "Groovy!" and **"Right on!"** a lot. Grateful Dead posters. **Psychedelic** lampshades.

So I was surprised. Her mother wore shorts and a tank top as she worked the pedal of a sewing machine with her bare foot. She was making a Russian peasant costume for a play to be presented in Denver. Mr. Caraway was on a stepladder outside, painting windowsills. No muttonchops; in fact, not much hair at all. The house itself could have been anyone's. Glossy bentwood furniture, throw rugs over hardwood floors, Southwest accents: an Anasazi-style wedding vase here, a Georgia O'Keeffe print there. Nothing to proclaim, "You see? She came from *here*."

Same with her room. Except for Cinnamon's blue and yellow plywood apartment in one corner, it might have belonged to any high school girl. I stood in the doorway.

"What?" she asked.

"I'm surprised," I said.

"At what?"

"I thought your room would be different."

....

a leftover hippie scene from the 1960s a group of young people who believed in peace and love

Right on! Yes!

Psychedelic Weird, Colorful

"How so?"

"I don't know. More . . . you."

She grinned. "Stacks of fillers? A card-making operation?"

"Something like that."

"That's my office," she said. She let Cinnamon out. He scurried under her bed. "This is my room."

"You have an office?"

"Yep." She stuck her foot under the bed. When it came out, Cinnamon was aboard. "I wanted to have a place all my own where I could go to work. So I got one."

Cinnamon scampered out of the room.

"Where is it?" I said.

She put her finger to her lips. "Secret."

"Bet I know one person who knows," I said.

She raised her eyebrows.

"Archie."

She smiled.

"He was talking about you," I said. "He likes you."

"**He means the world to me**," she said. "I think of him as my grandfather."

My inspection yielded two curious items. One was a wooden bowl half filled with sand-colored hair.

"Yours?" I said.

She nodded. "For birds looking for nest materials. I put it out in the spring. Been doing it since I was a little girl. **I got more business** up north than here."

The other item was on a bookshelf. It was a tiny wagon

....

He means the world to me He is very important to me

My inspection yielded two curious items. I found two strange things while I looked around.

I got more business More birds took my hair

about the size of my fist. It was made of wood and looked like it might have been an antique toy. It was piled high with pebbles. Several other pebbles lay about the wagon wheels.

I pointed to it. "You collecting stones, or what?"

"It's my happy wagon," she said. "Actually, it could **just as well** be called an unhappy wagon, but I prefer happy."

"So what's it all about?"

"It's about how I feel. When something makes me happy, I put a pebble in the wagon. If I'm unhappy, I take a pebble out. There are twenty pebbles in all."

I counted three on the shelf. "So there're seventeen in the wagon now, right?"

"Right."

"So that means, what, you're pretty happy?"

"Right again."

"What's the biggest number of pebbles ever in the wagon?"

She gave me a sly smile. "You're looking at it."

It didn't seem like just a pile of pebbles anymore.

"Usually," she said, "it's more balanced. **It hangs around** ten, a couple to one side or the other. Back and forth, back and forth. Like life."

"How close to empty did the wagon ever get?" I said.

"Oh . . . " She turned her face to the ceiling, closed her eyes. "Once, down to three."

I was shocked. "Really? You?"

She stared. "Why *not* me?"

"You don't seem the type."

....

just as well also

It hangs around There are usually

"What type is that?"

"I don't know . . ." I **groped** for the right words.

"The three-pebble type?" she offered.

I shrugged.

She picked up a pebble from the shelf and, with a grin, dropped it into the wagon. "Well, call me Miss Unpredictable."

I joined the family for dinner. Three of us had meatloaf. The fourth—guess who—was a **strict vegetarian**. She had tofu loaf.

Her parents called her "Stargirl" and "Star" as casually as if she were a Jennifer.

After dinner we sat on her front step. She had brought her camera out. Three little kids, two girls and a boy, were playing in a driveway across the street. She took several pictures of them.

"Why are you doing that?" I asked her.

"See the little boy in the red cap?" she said. "His name is Peter Sinkowitz. He's five years old. I'm **doing** his biography, sort of."

For the tenth time that day she had **caught me off guard**. "Biography?" Peter Sinkowitz was coasting down his driveway in a four-wheeled plastic banana; the two little girls were running, screaming after him. "Why would you want to do that?"

She snapped a picture. "Don't you wish somebody came up to you today and gave you a scrapbook called 'The Life of Leo Borlock'? And it's a record, like a journal, of what you did on

....

groped searched

strict vegetarian person who did not eat meat

doing creating, making

caught me off guard surprised me

such-and-such a date when you were little. From the days you can't remember anymore. And there's pictures, and even stuff that you dropped or threw away, like a candy wrapper. And it was all done by some neighbor across the street, and you didn't even know she was doing it. Don't you think when you're fifty or sixty you'd give a fortune to have such a thing?"

I thought about it. It was ten years since I had been six. It seemed like a century. She was right about one thing: I didn't remember much about those days. But I didn't really care either.

"No," I said, "I don't think so. And anyway, don't you think his parents are doing that? Family albums and all?"

One of the little girls managed to **wrest** the banana roadster away from Peter Sinkowitz. Peter started howling.

"I'm sure they are," she said, snapping another picture. "But those pictures and those moments are posed and smiling. They're not as real as this. Someday he's going to love this picture of himself bawling while a little girl rides off on his toy. I don't follow him around like we did Clarissa. I just **keep an eye out** for him, and a couple of times a week I jot down what I saw him doing that day. I'll do it for a few more years, then I'll give it to his parents to give to him when he's older and ready to appreciate it." A puzzled look came over her face. She poked me with her elbow. "What?"

"Huh?" I said.

"You're staring at me really funny. What is it?"

I blurted, **"Are you running for saint?"**

I regretted the words as soon as they left my lips. She just

....

wrest get, take

keep an eye out always look

Are you running for saint? Why are you trying to be so perfect?

looked at me, hurt in her eyes.

"Sorry," I said. "I didn't mean to sound nasty."

"How did you mean to sound?"

"Amazed, I guess."

"At what?"

I laughed. "What do you think? *You.*" I laughed again. I stood before the steps, facing her. "Look at you. It's Saturday. I've been with you all day, and you've spent the whole day doing stuff for other people. Or paying attention to other people. Or following other people. Or taking pictures of other people."

She looked up at me. The hurt was gone from her eyes, but not the **puzzlement**. She blinked. "So?"

"So . . . I don't know what I'm saying."

"Sounds like you're saying I'm obsessed with other people. Is that it?"

Maybe it was the angle, but her fawn's eyes, looking up at me, seemed larger than ever. I had to make an effort to keep my balance **lest I fall into them**. "You're different," I said, "that's for sure."

She batted her eyelids and gave me a **flirty** grin. "Don't you like different?"

"Sure I do," I said, maybe a little too quickly.

A look of sudden discovery brightened her face. She reached out with her foot and tapped my sneaker. "I know what your problem is."

"Really?" I said. "What?"

"You're jealous. You're upset because I'm paying all this

....

puzzlement confusion
lest I fall into them because I was feeling so much love
flirty playful, happy

136

attention to other people and not enough to you."

"Right," I sniffed. "I'm jealous of Peter Sinkowitz."

She stood. "You just want me all to yourself, don't you?" **She stepped into my space.** The tips of our noses were touching. "Don't you, Mr. Leo?" Her arms were around my neck.

We were on the sidewalk in front of her house, in full view. "What are you doing?" I said.

"I'm giving you some attention," she cooed. "Don't you want some attention?"

I was losing my battle for balance.

"I don't know," I heard myself say.

"You're really dumb," she whispered in my ear.

"Yeah?"

"Yeah. Why do you think there're eighteen pebbles in my wagon?" And then the last remaining space between our lips was gone and I was falling **headlong into her eyes**, right there on Palo Verde after dinner. And I can tell you, that was no saint kissing me.

....

She stepped into my space. She came closer to me.
I was losing my battle for balance. I felt strange.
headlong into her eyes in love

BEFORE YOU MOVE ON...

1. **Conclusions** Stargirl enjoys helping others. Why is Leo so surprised by this?

2. **Assumption** What does Leo assume about Stargirl's family? How does he change his mind?

LOOK AHEAD Read to page 157. Why does Leo start to avoid Stargirl?

23

Those were the best times, when we were alone, together, out of school. We took long walks around town and into the desert, to her enchanted place. We sat on park benches and people-watched. I introduced her to strawberry-banana smoothies. I borrowed the pickup and drove us to Red Rock and Glendale. On weekends we went to Archie's. On his back porch, we talked of a thousand things and laughed and **swooned** in pipesmoke and ate pizza. She presented her oratorical contest speech to Señor Saguaro. We never spoke of the shunning. I loved weekends.

But Mondays always followed Sundays.

And the shunning—it was clear now—had come to me. It was less absolute for me than for her, but it was there. I saw it in the eyes that shifted away from mine, the shoulders that turned, the chatter that seemed less loud around me now than before. I fought it. **I tested its limits.** In the courtyard, between classes, in the lunchroom, I called out to others just to see if they would respond. When someone turned and nodded, I felt grateful. If someone spoke to me, especially if I had not spoken first, I wanted to cry. I had never realized how much I needed the attention of others to **confirm my own presence**.

I told myself that the shunning was more painful for me than for Stargirl. I told myself that she was too busy being herself to notice that she was being ignored—and in fact, she

....

swooned felt dizzy

I tested its limits. I tried to get people to talk to me.

confirm my own presence make me feel like a real person continued to give birthday people a ukulele serenade and to decorate her desk and to distribute assorted kindnesses. I told myself that even if she did notice, she wouldn't care.

I understood why this was happening to me. In the eyes of the student body, she was part of my identity. I was "her boyfriend." I was Mr. Stargirl.

Students said things. Not to me, not directly, but tuned for me to overhear even as they pretended I was nowhere near. They said she **was a self-centered spotlight hogger**. They said she thought she was some kind of saint—I cringed at that—and that she was better than the rest of us. They said she wanted everyone else to feel guilty for not being as nice and wonderful as she was. They said she was a phony.

Most of all, they said she was the reason why the Mica Electrons were not soon to become Arizona state basketball champions. Kevin had been right: when she started cheering for other teams, she did something bad to her own team. To see one of their own **priming the opposition** did something to the team's morale that hours of practice could not overcome. And the last straw—everyone seemed to agree—was the Sun Valley game, when Stargirl rushed across the court to aid Kovac, the Sun Valley star. All of this was affirmed by our own star, Ardsley himself, who said that when he saw a Mica cheerleader giving comfort to the enemy, **the heart went out of him**. She was why they lost the next game so miserably to Red Rock. They hated her for it, and they would never forgive.

Unlike Stargirl, I was aware of the constant anger of our

....

was a self-centered spotlight hogger only cared about herself and needed a lot of attention

priming the opposition helping the other team

the heart went out of him he gave up

schoolmates, **seething** like snakes under a porch. In fact, I was not only aware of it, but at times I also understood their point of view. There were even moments when **something small and huddled** within me agreed with it. But then I would see her smile and take a swan dive into her eyes, and the bad moment would be gone.

I saw. I heard. I understood. I suffered. But **whose sake** was I suffering for? I kept thinking of Señor Saguaro's question: *Whose affection do you value more, hers or the others'?*

I became angry. I resented having to choose. I refused to choose. I imagined my life without her and without them, and I didn't like it either way. I pretended it would not always be like this. In the magical moonlight of my bed at night, I pretended she would become more like them and they would become more like her, and in the end I would have it all.

Then she did something that made pretending impossible.

....

seething angry
something small and huddled a small feeling
whose sake who

24

"Roadrunner."

No one said the word to me directly, but I kept hearing it since I arrived at school one day, several days after the kiss on the sidewalk. **It seemed more dropped behind than spoken, so that I kept walking into it:**

"Roadrunner."

Was there something on the plywood roadrunner that I should read?

I had study hall coming up third period; I'd look into it then. In the meantime, I had second-period Spanish. As I headed for my seat, I looked out the window, which faced the courtyard. There was something written on the roadrunner, all right, but I wouldn't have to go outside to read it. I could read it from here. I could have read it from a low-flying airplane. White paper—no, it was a bedsheet—covered the whole bird. Painted on the sheet in broad red brush strokes was a Valentine heart enclosing the words:

STARGIRL LOVES LEO

My first **impulse** was to drag the Spanish teacher to the window and say, "Look! She loves me!" My second impulse was

---

It seemed more dropped behind than spoken, so that I kept walking into it: People kept saying it so that I would hear it:

impulse desire, thought

to run outside and rip the sign away.

Until now, I had never been the target of her public extravagance. I felt a sudden, strange kinship with Hillari Kimble: I understood why she had commanded Stargirl not to sing to her. I felt **spotlighted on a bare stage**.

I couldn't concentrate on my schoolwork or anything else. I was a mess.

At lunch that day, I was afraid to look at her. I counted one blessing: I had not yet worked up the nerve to sit with her each day. I kept **stoking** my conversation with Kevin. I felt her presence, her eyes, three tables to my left. I knew she was sitting there with Dori Dilson, the only friend who had not deserted her. I felt the faint tug of her gaze on the back of my neck. Ignoring my wishes, my head turned on its own and there she was: smiling **to beat the band**, waving grandly, and—horrors!—blowing me a kiss. I snapped my head back and dragged Kevin out of the lunchroom.

When I finally dared to look again at the courtyard, I found that someone had torn the sign away. Thumbtacks at the corners pinned four white scraps of bedsheet to the plywood.

I managed to avoid her by taking different routes between classes, but she found me after school, came shouting after me as I tried to **slink away**: "Leo! Leo!"

She ran up to me, breathless, bursting, her eyes sparkling in the sun. "Did you see it?"

I nodded. I kept walking.

"Well?" She was hopping beside me, punching my shoulder.

....

spotlighted on a bare stage like everyone was looking at me
stoking continuing
to beat the band happily, proudly
slink away get away quickly and quietly

"Wha'd you think?"

What could I say? I didn't want to hurt her feelings. I just shrugged.

"Wow. That impressed, huh?" She was mocking me. She reached into her bag and pulled out her rat. "Maybe he's shy, Cinnamon. Maybe he'll tell you how thrilled he was to see the sign." She set him on my shoulder.

I yelped. I swept the rat off and sent him flying to the ground.

She scooped him up and stroked him, all the while staring at me **dumbstruck**. I could not face her. I turned and walked on alone.

She called, "I guess you don't want to hear me practice my speech, huh?"

I did not answer. I did not look back.

The next day I faced the full impact of the sign. I thought I had truly suffered **from the spillover of Stargirl's shunning**, but that was nothing now that **the full torrent** was turned on me.

Of course Kevin—thankfully—talked to me; so did a few other friends. But the rest was silence, a second desert imposed upon the one I already lived in, where "Hi" was as rare as rain. I came to the courtyard in the morning before opening bell, and all I saw were backs of heads. People shouldered past me, calling others. Doors closed in my face. There was laughter, there was fun, but it skipped over me like a flat stone on water.

One morning as I was running a teacher's errand, I saw

....

dumbstruck shocked, confused

from the spillover of Stargirl's shunning by being ignored along with Stargirl

the full torrent all of the attention and anger

someone named Renshaw walking across the courtyard. I barely knew the kid, but we were the only two in the courtyard at that moment, and I had to, so to speak, **touch the stove that I knew was hot**. "Renshaw!" I called. There was no other voice but mine. *"Renshaw!"* He never turned, never **wavered**, never slowed down. He kept walking away from me, opened a door, and was gone.

So what? I kept telling myself. What do you care? You never speak to each other. What's Renshaw to you?

But I did care. I couldn't help myself from caring. At that moment, there was nothing more I wanted in the world than a **nod** from Renshaw. I prayed that the door would burst open and he would be there saying, "Sorry, Borlock, I wasn't listening. What did you want?" But the door stayed closed, and I knew what it felt like to be invisible.

"I'm invisible," I said to Kevin at lunch. "Nobody hears me. Nobody sees me. I'm the friggin' invisible man."

Kevin just looked at his lunch and wagged his head.

"How long's it going to go on?" I demanded.

He shrugged.

"What did I *do*?" My voice was louder than I intended.

He chewed. He stared. At last he said, "You know what you did."

....

touch the stove that I knew was hot know for sure that no one would talk to me

wavered seemed like he might stop

nod friendly gesture

I stared at him like he was crazy. **I badgered him some more.** But of course he was perfectly right. I knew exactly what I had done. I had **linked** myself to an unpopular person. That was my crime.

....

I badgered him some more. I asked him more questions.
linked connected

25

Days passed. I continued to avoid Stargirl. I wanted her. I wanted them. It seemed I could not have both, so I did nothing. I ran and hid.

But she did not give up on me. **She hunted me down.** She found me in the TV studio after school one day. I felt fingers slipping down the back of my neck, grabbing my collar, pulling me backward. The crew was staring. "Mr. Borlock," I heard her say, "we need to talk." Her voice told me she was not smiling. She released my collar. I followed her out of the room.

In the courtyard a couple **cooing** on the bench beneath the palmetto saw us coming and bolted, so that's where we sat.

"So," she said, "are we breaking up already?"

"I don't want to," I said.

"So why are you hiding from me?"

Forced to face her, forced to talk, I felt my **gumption** rising. "Something's gotta change," I said. "That's all I know."

"You mean like change clothes? Or change a tire? Should I change a tire on my bike? Would that do it?"

"You're not funny. You know what I mean."

She saw I was upset. Her face got serious.

"People aren't talking to me," I said. I stared at her. I wanted it to **sink in.** "People I've known ever since we moved here. They don't talk to me. They don't *see* me."

She reached out and lightly rubbed the back of my hand

She hunted me down. She looked everywhere for me.

cooing being romantic

gumption courage, nerve

sink in affect her seriously

with her fingertip. Her eyes were sad. "I'm sorry people don't see you. It's no fun not being seen, is it?"

I pulled my hand away. "Well, you tell me what it's like. Doesn't it bother you that nobody talks to you?" It was the first time I had **openly mentioned** the shunning to her.

She smiled. "Dori talks to me. You talk to me. Archie talks to me. My family talks to me. Cinnamon talks to me. Señor Saguaro talks to me. *I* talk to me." She cocked her head and stared at me, waiting for a responding smile. I didn't give it. "Are *you* going to stop talking to me?"

"That's not the question," I said.

"What *is* the question?"

"The question is"—I tried to **read her face** but I could not— "**what makes you tick?**"

"Now I'm a *clock!*"

I turned away. "See, I can't talk to you. It's all just a big joke."

She put my face between her hands and turned me to her. I hoped people were not watching from the windows. "Okay, serious now. Go ahead, ask me the tick question again. Or any other, any question at all."

I shook my head. "You just don't care, do you?"

That **stumped** her. "Care? Leo, how can you say I don't care? You've gone with me to places. We've delivered cards and flowers. How can you say—"

"That's not what I mean. I mean you don't care what people think."

....

openly mentioned talked aloud about
read her face understand her thoughts
what makes you tick? what is important to you?
stumped confused

"I care what *you* think. I care—"

"I know—you care what Cinnamon and Señor Saguaro think. I'm talking about the school, the town. I'm talking about everybody."

She sniffed around the word. "Everybody?"

"Right. You don't seem to care what everybody thinks. You don't seem to *know* what everybody thinks. You—"

She broke in: "Do you?"

I thought for a moment. I nodded sharply. "Yeah. Yeah, I think I do know. **I'm in touch with** everybody. I'm one of them. How could I not know?"

"And it matters?"

"Sure, it matters. Look"—I waved my arm at the school around us— "look what's happening. Nobody talks to us. You can't just not **give a crap** what anybody thinks. You can't just cheer for the other team and expect your own school to love you for it." Words that I had been thinking for weeks **rolled off my tongue** now. "Kovac—Kovac, for God's sake. What was *that* all about?"

She was baffled. "Who's Kovac?"

"Kovac. The guy from Sun Valley. The basketball star. The guy who broke his ankle."

She was still baffled. "What about him?"

"What about him? What about *you*? What were you doing out there on the floor with him with his head in your lap?"

"He was in pain."

"He was the *enemy*, Stargirl! Susan. Whatever. The *enemy*!"

....

She sniffed around the word. She did not know how to respond.

I'm in touch with I talk to

give a crap care

rolled off my tongue were easy to say

She stared dumbly back at me. She had blinked at "Susan." "There were a thousand Sun Valley people there. He had his *own* people to take care of him, his *own* coaches, his *own* teammates, his *own* cheerleaders' laps. And you had *your* own team to worry about." I was screeching. I got up and walked away. I came back, leaned into her. "Why?" I said. "Why didn't you just let him be taken care of by his own people?"

She looked at me for a long time, as if in my face she could find herself explained. "I don't know," she said dimly at last. "I didn't think. I just did."

I pulled back. I was tempted to say, *Well, I hope you're satisfied, because they hate you for what you did*, but I didn't **have the heart**.

Now I was feeling sorry for her. I sat back down beside her. I took her hand. I smiled. I spoke as gently as I could. "Stargirl, you just can't do things the way you do. If you weren't stuck in a homeschool all your life, you'd understand. You can't just wake up in the morning and say you don't care what the rest of the world thinks."

Her eyes were wide, her voice **peepy** like a little girl's. "You can't?"

"Not unless you want to be a **hermit**."

She flicked the hem of her skirt at my sneaker, dusting it. "But how do you **keep track of the rest of the world**? Sometimes I can hardly keep track of myself."

"It's not something you even have to think about," I said. "You just know. Because you're connected."

....

have the heart want to hurt her feelings
peepy high-pitched
hermit person who spends all their time alone
keep track of the rest of the world understand others

On the ground her bag shifted slightly: Cinnamon was stirring. Stargirl's face went through a series of expressions, ending with **a pout and a sudden sobby outburst**: "I'm not connected!" She reached out to me and we hugged on the bench in the courtyard and walked home together.

We continued this conversation for the next couple of days. I explained the ways of people to her. I said you can't cheer for everybody. She said why not? I said a person belongs to a group, you can't belong to everyone. She said why not? I said you can't just **barge into** the funeral of a perfect stranger. She said why not? I said you just can't. She said why? I said because. I said you have to respect other people's privacy, there's such a thing as not being welcome. I said not everybody likes having somebody with a ukulele sing "Happy Birthday" to them. They don't? she said.

This group thing, I said, it's very strong. It's probably an instinct. You find it everywhere, from little groups like families to big ones like a town or school, to really big ones like a whole country. How about really, *really* big ones, she said, like a planet? Whatever, I said. The point is, in a group everybody acts pretty much the same, that's kind of how the group holds itself together. Everybody? she said. Well, mostly, I said. That's what jails and mental hospitals are for, to keep it that way. You think I should be in jail? she said. I think you should try to be more like the rest of us, I said.

Why? she said.

....

a pout and a sudden sobby outburst her crying
barge into go to

Because, I said.

Tell me, she said.

It's hard, I said.

Say it, she said.

Because nobody likes you, I said. That's why. Nobody likes you.

Nobody? she said. Her eyes **covered me like the sky**. *Nobody?*

I tried to **play dumb**, but that wasn't working. Hey, I said, don't look at me. We're talking about them. *Them*. If it was up to me, I wouldn't change a thing. You're fine with me the way you are. But we're not alone, are we? We live in a world of them, like it or not.

That's where I tried to keep it, on them. I didn't mention myself. I didn't say do it for me. I didn't say if you don't change you can forget about me. I never said that.

Two days later Stargirl **vanished**.

....

covered me like the sky looked big
play dumb act like I was not sure
vanished disappeared

26

Usually I saw her in the courtyard before school, but that day
I didn't. Usually I passed her between classes at least once or
twice before lunch. Not that day. In fact, when I looked over to
her table at lunch, there was Dori Dilson, as usual, but someone
else was sitting with her. No Stargirl in sight.

Coming out of the lunchroom, I heard laughter behind me.
And then a voice, Stargirl's: "What do you have to do to get
somebody's attention around here?"

I turned, but it wasn't her. The girl standing, grinning in
front of me wore jeans and sandals, had burnt-red nails and
lipstick, painted eyes, finger rings, toe rings, hoop earrings I
could put my hand through, hair . . .

I gawked as students swarmed past. She made a clownish
grin. She was beginning to look vaguely familiar. **Tentatively**
I whispered, "Stargirl?"

She batted her chocolaty eyelashes. "Stargirl? What kind of
name is that? My name is Susan."

And **just like that**, Stargirl was gone, replaced by Susan.
Susan Julia Caraway. The girl she might have been all along.

I couldn't take my eyes off her. She cradled her books in
her arms. The sunflower canvas bag was gone. The rat was
gone. The ukulele was gone. She turned around slowly for my
openmouthed, dumbstruck inspection. Nothing goofy, nothing
different could I see. She looked magnificently, wonderfully,

---

Tentatively Doubtfully
just like that instantly

gloriously ordinary. She looked just like a hundred other girls at Mica High. Stargirl had vanished into **a sea of *them***, and I was thrilled. She slid a stick of chewing gum into her mouth and chewed away noisily. She winked at me. She reached out and **tweaked** my cheek the way my grandmother would and said, "What's up, cutie?" I grabbed her, right there outside the lunchroom in the swarming mob. I didn't care if others were watching. In fact, I hoped they were. I grabbed her and squeezed her. I had never been so happy and so proud in my life.

We sailed through time. We held hands in the hallways, on the stairs, in the courtyard. In the lunchroom I grabbed her and pulled her over to our table. I looked to invite Dori Dilson, too, but she was gone. I sat there grinning while Kevin and Susan gabbed and gossiped over their sandwiches. They joked about her disastrous appearance on *Hot Seat*. Susan suggested that I should go on *Hot Seat* one of these days, and Kevin said no, he's too shy, and I said not anymore, and we all laughed.

And it was true. I didn't walk, I strutted. I was Susan Caraway's boyfriend. I. Me. Really? *That* Susan Caraway? The one with the tiny barrettes and toe rings? Yep, that's the one, my girlfriend. Call me Mr. Susan.

I started saying "we" instead of "I," as in "We'll meet you there" or "We like fajitas."

Whenever I could, I said her name out loud, like blowing bubbles. The rest of the time I said it to myself.

Susan . . . Susan . . .

....

a sea of *them* the crowd
tweaked pinched
We sailed through time. Time seemed to pass quickly.

We did our homework together. We hung out with Kevin. Instead of following strangers around, we went to the movies and plunged our hands together into the six-dollar Super Tub of popcorn. Instead of shopping for African violets, we shopped for Cinnabons and licked icing from each other's fingers.

We went into Pisa Pizza. We walked past the bulletin board inside the door. We shared a pizza: half pepperoni, half anchovies.

"Anchovies, ugh," I said.

"What's wrong with anchovies?" she said.

"How can you eat them? Nobody eats anchovies."

I was sort of kidding, but her face was serious. "Nobody?"

"Nobody I know."

She picked the anchovies from her slices and dumped them into her water glass.

I tried to stop her. "Hey—"

She pushed my hand away. She dropped the last anchovy into the glass. "I don't want to be like nobody."

On the way out, we ignored the bulletin board.

She **was mad for** shopping. It was as if she had just discovered clothes. She bought shirts and pants and shorts and costume jewelry and makeup. I began to notice that the items of clothing had one thing in common: they all had the designer's name **plastered prominently on** them. She seemed to buy not for color or style but for designer label size.

She constantly quizzed me about what other kids would do, would buy, would say, would think. She invented a fictitious

....

was mad for loved

plastered prominently on all over

person whom she called Evelyn Everybody. "Would Evelyn like this?" "Would Evelyn do that?"

Sometimes she **misfired**, as with laughing. For several days she was **on a laughing jag**. She didn't just laugh, she boomed. Heads turned in the lunchroom. I was trying to work up the nerve to say something when she looked at Kevin and me and said, "Would Evelyn laugh this much?" Kevin stared at his sandwich. I sheepishly shook my head. The laughing stopped, and from that moment on she did a perfect imitation of a sullen, pout-lipped teenager.

In every way she seemed to be a typical, ordinary, everyday, run-of-the-mill teenager.

And it wasn't working.

At first I neither noticed nor much cared that the shunning continued. I was too busy being happy that she was, as I saw it, now one of us. My only regret was that we could not play the basketball season over again. **In my mind's eye**, I pictured her aiming her incredible zeal and energy exclusively at the Electrons. We could have won games on her cheering alone.

It was she who said it first: "They still don't like me." We were standing outside the TV studio after school. As usual, people were passing by as if we weren't there. Her lip quivered. "What am I doing wrong?" Tears made her eyes even larger.

I squeezed her hand. I told her to give it some time. I pointed out that the state basketball finals would take place in Phoenix that Saturday, and that would end the season and clear

....

misfired still did the wrong thing
on a laughing jag laughing too much
In my mind's eye In my imagination

the way for her cheerleading crimes to be forgotten.

Her mascara was muddy. I had seen her sad many times before, but always for someone else. This was different. This was for herself, and **I was powerless to help**. I could not find **it in me** to cheer up the cheerleader.

That night we did homework together at her house. I **ducked** into her room to check out her happy wagon. There were only two stones in it.

When I came to school next day, there was something different about the buzz in the courtyard. The arriving students were milling about, some roaming at random, some in clusters, but as I approached, there seemed to be a distinct clearing around the palmetto. I wandered in that direction, and through the crowd I could see that someone—Susan—was seated on the bench. She sat upright and smiling. She was holding a foot-long stick shaped like a claw on one end. Around her neck, dangling on a string, was a sign that read: TALK TO ME AND I'LL SCRATCH YOUR BACK. She was getting no takers. No one was within twenty feet of her.

Quickly I turned away. I walked back through the crowd. I pretended I was looking for someone. I pretended I hadn't seen. And prayed for the bell to ring.

When I saw her later that morning, the sign was gone. She said nothing about it. Neither did I.

Next morning she came running at me in the courtyard. Her eyes were bright for the first time in days. She grabbed me with both hands and shook me. "It's going to be okay! It's going

....

I was powerless to help I could not help her

it in me the energy

ducked snuck; went quickly

to end! **I had a vision!**"

She told me about it. She had gone to her enchanted place after dinner the day before, and that's where the vision had come to her. She had seen herself returning in triumph from the Arizona state oratorical contest. She had won first prize. Best in the state. When she returned, she **got a hero's welcome**. The whole school greeted her in the parking lot, just like in the assembly film. There were streamers and confetti and tooting kazoos and horns blaring, and the mayor and city council were **on hand**, and they had a parade right then and there, and she rode high on the back seat of a convertible and held her winner's silver plate up for all to see, and the happy faces of her classmates flashed in the sparkling trophy. She told me this, and she threw up her arms and shouted, "I'm going to be popular!"

The state contest was a week away. Every day she practiced her speech. One day she called over little Peter Sinkowitz and his playmates and presented the speech to us from her front steps. We applauded and whistled. She bowed **grandly**, and I, too, began to see her vision. I saw the streamers flying and I heard the crowd cheering, and I believed.

....

I had a vision! I saw the future!
got a hero's welcome was celebrated
on hand there
grandly proudly, deeply

BEFORE YOU MOVE ON...

1. **Conflict** Everyone is avoiding Leo, so he tries to change Stargirl. Why doesn't this solve his problem?

2. **Comparisons** How is Susan different from Stargirl?

LOOK AHEAD Read pages 158–174 to see if Susan finally becomes popular.

" . . . and our best wishes go with you, Susan Caraway."

The PA announcement echoed through the school lobby, and we were off to Phoenix. The driver was Mr. McShane, Mica High's faculty representative to the state contest. Susan and I sat in the back. Susan's parents were driving their own car and would meet us in Phoenix.

As we pulled out of the parking lot, she wagged a finger in my face. "Don't get **a big head**, mister. I was allowed to invite two friends along. You weren't the only one I asked."

"So who was the other?" I said.

"Dori."

"Well, then," I said, "I think I'll go for the big head. Dori isn't another guy."

She grinned. "No, she's not one of those." Suddenly she unbuckled her seat belt—we each had a back window. "Mr. McShane," she announced, "I'm moving over so I can sit close to Leo. He's so cute, I can't help myself."

In the rearview mirror, the teacher's eyes **crinkled**. "Whatever you like, Susan. It's your day."

She slid over and fastened herself into the middle belt. She jabbed me. "Hear that? It's my day. I get whatever I want."

"So," I said, "what happened when you asked Dori Dilson?"

"She said no. She's mad at me."

"I could tell."

----

a big head too proud; too conceited

crinkled showed he was smiling

"Ever since I became Susan. She thinks I **betrayed** myself. She just doesn't understand how important it is to be popular."

I wasn't sure what to say to that. I was feeling a little uneasy. Fortunately, wondering what to say wasn't much of a problem for me during that two-hour ride, because Susan chattered away like the old Stargirl the whole time.

"But I know Dori," she said, "and I'll tell you one thing."

"What's that?"

"She'll be in the front of the mob cheering for me when we get back tomorrow."

I later found out that after we left the school, the principal had spoken again on the PA. He announced our expected time of return on Saturday and suggested that everyone be on hand to meet us, win or lose.

Losing, as it turned out, **never occurred to the contestant herself.**

"Would you do a favor for me?" she said.

I told her sure.

"That big silver plate that goes to the winner? I'm such a klutz with dishes at home. Would you hold it for me when the crowd **rushes** us? I'm afraid I'll drop it."

I stared at her. "What crowd? What rush?"

"In the school parking lot. When we get back tomorrow. There's always a crowd waiting for the returning hero. Remember the film at school? My vision?" She cocked her head and peered into my eyes. She rapped my forehead with her knuckle. "Hello in there. Anybody home?"

....

betrayed am not being

never occurred to the contestant herself was not something Susan thought was going to happen

rushes comes up to

"Oh," I said. "*That* crowd."

She nodded. "Exactly. Of course, we'll be safe as long as we're in the car. But once we get out, who knows what will happen. Crowds can get pretty wild. Right, Mr. McShane?"

The teacher nodded. "So I hear."

She spoke to me as if instructing a first-grader. "Leo, this has never happened in Mica before, having a winner of the Arizona state oratorical contest. One of their very own. When they hear about it, they're going to **go bananas**. And when they **get a gander at** me and that trophy—" She rolled her eyes and whistled. "I just hope they don't get out of hand."

"The police will keep them in line," I said. "Maybe they'll call out the National Guard."

She stared wide-eyed. "You think?" She didn't realize I was kidding. "Well," she said, "I'm really not afraid for myself. I won't mind a little jostling. Do you think they'll jostle, Mr. McShane?"

In the mirror his eyes shifted to us. "Never can tell."

"And if they want to carry me around on their shoulders, that's okay, too. But they better not"—she poked me with her finger—"better *not* mess with my trophy. That's why *you*"—another poke—"are going to hold it. Tight."

I wished Mr. McShane would say something. "Susan," I said, "did you ever hear of **counting your chickens**?"

"**Before they hatch**, you mean?"

"Exactly."

"I hear you're not supposed to."

....

go bananas be very excited and happy

get a gander at see

counting your chickens expecting too much

Before they hatch Too soon

160

"Exactly."

She nodded thoughtfully. "Never made much sense to me. I mean, if you *know* **they're going to hatch, why not count them**?"

"Because you can't know," I said. "There're no guarantees. I hate to **break this to you**, but you're not the only person in the contest. Somebody else *could* win. You *could* lose. It's possible."

She thought about that for a moment, then shook her head. "Nope. Not possible. So . . . " She threw up her arms and smiled hugely. "Why wait to feel great? Celebrate now, that's my **motto**." She nuzzled into me. "What's yours, big boy?"

"Don't count your chickens," I said.

She shuddered mockingly. "Ouuu. You're such a poop, Leo. What's your motto, Mr. McShane?"

"Drive carefully," he said, "you may have a winner in the car."

That set her off howling.

"Mr. McShane," I said, "you're not helping."

"Sorry," he lied.

I just looked at her. "You're going to be in a state contest," I said. "Aren't you just a little bit nervous?"

The smile vanished. "Yes, I am. I'm a lot nervous. I just hope things don't get out of hand when we get back to the school. I've never been adored by mobs of people before. I'm not sure how I'm going to react. I hope I don't get a big head. Do you think I'm the big-head type, Mr. McShane?"

I raised my hand. "Can I answer that?"

....

they're going to hatch, why not count them something good is going to happen, why not get excited

break this to you tell you this

motto special saying or statement

"I think your head is just fine," said the teacher.

She jabbed me with her elbow. "Hear that, Mr. Know-it-all?" She gave me her smug face, which promptly disappeared as she thrust up her arms and yelped, "They're going to love me!"

Mr. McShane wagged his head and chuckled. Silently I gave up.

She pointed out the window. "Look, even the desert is celebrating."

It seemed to be true. The normally dull cacti and scrub were splashed with April colors, as if a great painter had passed over the landscape with a brush, dabbing yellow here, red there.

Susan strained against her seat belt. "Mr. McShane, can we stop here, just for a minute? Please?" When the teacher hesitated, she added, "You said it's my day. I get whatever I want."

The car **coasted** to a stop along the gravelly roadside. In a moment, she was out the door and bounding across the desert. She skipped and whirled and cartwheeled among the prickly natives. She bowed to a yucca, **waltzed** with a saguaro. She plucked a red blossom from a barrel cactus and fixed it in her hair. She practiced her smile and her nod and her wave—one-hand, two-hand—to the adoring mob at her hero's welcome. She snapped a needle from a cactus and **with the slapstick pantomime of** a circus clown pretended to pick her teeth with it.

Mr. McShane and I were leaning on the car, laughing, when suddenly she stopped, cocked her head, and stared off in

....

coasted came slowly

waltzed danced

with the slapstick pantomime of like

another direction. She stayed like that, stone still, for a good two minutes, then abruptly turned and came back to the car.

Her face was thoughtful. "Mr. McShane," she said as the teacher drove off, "do you know any extinct birds?"

"Passenger pigeon," he said. "That's probably the best known. They say there used to be so many of them they would darken the sky when they flew over. And the moa."

"Moa?"

"Huge bird."

"Like a condor?" I said.

He chuckled. "A condor wouldn't come up to its knee. Make an ostrich look small. Twelve, thirteen feet tall. Maybe the biggest bird ever. Couldn't fly. Lived in New Zealand. **Died out** hundreds of years ago. **Killed off by people.**"

"Half their size," said Susan.

Mr. McShane nodded. "Mm. I wrote a report about moas in grade school. I thought they were the neatest thing."

Susan's eyes were glistening. "Did moas have a voice?"

The teacher thought about it. "I don't know. I don't know if anybody knows."

Susan looked out the window at the passing desert. "I heard a mockingbird back there. And it made me think of something Archie said."

"Mr. Brubaker?" said Mr. McShane.

"Yes. He said he believes mockingbirds may do more than imitate other birds. I mean, other *living birds*. He thinks they may also imitate the sounds of birds that are no longer around.

Died out Became extinct

Killed off by people. They were hunted until none were left.

He thinks the sounds of extinct birds are passed down the years from mockingbird to mockingbird."

"Interesting thought," said Mr. McShane.

"He says when a mockingbird sings, **for all we know it's pitching fossils into the air**. He says who knows what songs of ancient creatures we may be hearing out there."

The words of Archie Brubaker settled over the silence in the car. As if **reading my thoughts**, Mr. McShane turned off the air conditioner and **powered down** the windows. Hair blew in a faint, smoky scent of mesquite.

After a while I felt the touch of Susan's hand. Her fingers wove through mine.

"Mr. McShane," she cooed, "we're holding hands in the back seat."

"Uh-oh," he said, "hormonal teenagers."

"Don't you think he's cute, Mr. McShane?"

"I never really thought about it," said the teacher.

"Well, look," she said. She grabbed my face in her hand and pulled it forward. The teacher's eyes considered me briefly in the rearview mirror.

"You're right. He's adorable."

Susan released my blushing face. "Told you. Don't you just love him?"

"I wouldn't go that far."

....

for all we know it's pitching fossils into the air it might be singing the songs of extinct birds

reading my thoughts he knew what I was thinking

powered down opened

A minute later: "Mr. McSha-ane . . . " Now I felt something in my ear. "I'm putting my finger in his ear . . . "

This sort of silliness went on until we **rounded a mesa** and saw the brown mist on the horizon that **announced our approach to** the city of Phoenix.

....

rounded a mesa came around a corner

announced our approach to told us that we had arrived in

28

Her parents met us in the lobby of the hotel where Susan,
Mr. McShane, and I each had a room for the night. After
we **checked in**, the five of us ate a buffet lunch in the hotel
restaurant. Then we watched Susan board a bus that would
take her and eighteen other contestants to Phoenix West High
School. There were thirty-eight contestants; nineteen had
already given their speeches that morning.

By the end of the afternoon, ten finalists would be chosen.
The finals would take place that evening.

To be honest, none of us was surprised that Susan **made the
cut**. She was incredibly good. The surprise was this: her speech
was new. It was not the one she had given at Mica High. It was
not the one she had been practicing for weeks in front of me
and Peter Sinkowitz and assorted saguaros. It was not the one I
had heard just the day before.

But it was wonderful.

There were some elements of the old speech in it, and
much that was as new as that morning. Like a butterfly, her
words fluttered from image to image. She swung from the
distant past (Barney, Archie's Paleocene rodent skull) to the
present (Cinnamon) to the distant future (the death of the
sun). From the most ordinary here (the old man nodding off
on the bench at Tudor Village) to the most extraordinary
there (a newly discovered galaxy ninety percent to the end of

....

checked in signed in as guests
made the cut was chosen for the finals

the universe). She touched on silver lunch trucks and designer labels and enchanted places, and when she said her best friend gave her pet rat a ride on his shoulder, tears came to my eyes. It was a jumble, it was a mishmash, and somehow she pulled it all together, somehow she **threaded every different thing through the voice of a solitary mockingbird singing in the desert.** She called her speech "I Might Have Heard a Moa."

The auditorium was half full, mostly with small groups of students and parents from the competing schools. After a contestant finished, his or her supporters whistled and whooped, as if doing so would influence the judges. The rest was polite applause.

When Susan finished, the four of us managed a modest cheer, but that was about it. No whistles, no whoops. I think we were made of more timid stuff than the speechmaker herself.

Back at the hotel Mr. McShane and I mobbed her, if two can he a mob. Her parents were more reserved. They were full of smiles and "well dones," but they seemed no more surprised at her success than Susan did.

When the adults went off to the gift shop, I had her to myself. I said, "Where did *that* come from?"

She grinned. "Did you like it?"

"Sure, but it's not what I've been hearing for the last month. What were you doing, practicing a secret speech on the side?"

The grin got wider. "Nope. That was the first time I heard it, too."

I stared at her. Slowly her words sank in. "Let me get this

....

threaded every different thing through the voice of a solitary mockingbird singing in the desert made everything connect straight. You're saying you just made it up this morning?"

"I'm saying I didn't even make it up. It was just there. All I did was open my mouth and let it out." She held both hands out to me and snapped her fingers. **"Presto!"**

I gaped at her. "What are you going to say tonight?"

She threw out her arms: "Who knows?"

The five of us ate an early dinner in the hotel restaurant. Afterward, we waited in the lobby while Susan changed clothes. She stepped off the elevator wearing a peach-colored pantsuit. She slinked across the lobby, modeling for us. She sat on her mother's lap and said, "My personal seamstress made it for me." We applauded lightly and sent her off on the bus.

The general public was invited to the evening show, and the auditorium was packed. People stood in back. Down front, a high school orchestra played **rousing** music by John Philip Sousa. The ten contestants sat onstage. Seven were boys. All of the contestants appeared to be grim and nervous, stiff as manikins, except for Susan, who was **bending the ear of** the boy sitting next to her. He nodded occasionally but kept his eyes and spine at attention and obviously wished that she would shut up. Susan's parents chuckled knowingly at her behavior, while I tried to **disguise a stab** of jealousy.

One by one the contestants took the long walk to center stage to give their speeches. The applause was equally hearty for all. A grade school girl in a frilly white dress handed each

....

"Presto!" "Magic!"
rousing exciting
bending the ear of talking a lot to
disguise a stab hide a feeling

contestant a bouquet of roses, yellow for the girls, red for the boys. While the girls cradled their roses, the boys looked at them as if they were **hand grenades**.

Susan was next to last to speak. When her name was called, she bounced up from her chair and practically ran to the microphone. She did a sprightly pirouette, a curtsy, waved her hand in a window-washer motion, and said, "Hi." Accustomed to seeing stiff, mortified contestants, the audience responded with uncertain **titters**. They didn't know what to make of this unconventional teenager any more than we had on the first day of school. Several bold souls said "Hi" and waved back.

She did not begin, at least not in the usual sense. There was no ringing preamble. She merely stood there comfortably chatting away as if we were all on rocking chairs on her front porch. **Murmur drifted toward the ceiling**; people were waiting for her to get started. The murmur subsided as it occurred to them that this was it and they were missing it. The quiet that then fell over the auditorium was absolute. I was more tuned in to the audience than to the speaker, and if for the last five minutes of her talk anyone was breathing, I could not detect it. When she finished with barely a whisper—"Can you hear it?"—and leaned with her cupped hand to her ear, fifteen hundred people seemed to inch forward, straining to hear. There were ten seconds of purest stillness. Then she turned abruptly and went back to her chair. Still there was no reaction. What's going on? I wondered. She sat forward in her chair, her

....

hand grenades small bombs

titters laughter

Murmur drifted toward the ceiling People did not know this was her speech hands folded **primly** in her lap. And then it came, suddenly, explosively, as if everyone **had awakened at once**. We were all on our feet, clapping and shouting and whistling. I found myself sobbing. The cheering was as wild as that of the crowd at a championship basketball game.

....

primly politely, properly

had awakened at once was suddenly awake

29

She won. As she had said she would.

The silver plate they gave her twinkled like a starburst in a galaxy of flashing cameras. Two TV crews **washed her in lights** and interviewed her backstage. Strangers mobbed her, citizens of Phoenix gushing, telling her they had been coming to the contest for years and had never heard anything like it. Schoolchildren thrust programs in her face for autographs. Every parent wanted her for a daughter, every teacher for a student.

She was so happy, she was so proud. She yelped and cried when she saw us. She hugged each of us in turn, and I thought she would squeeze the breath out of me.

Back at the hotel everyone already seemed to know: the doorman, the desk manager, the people in the lobby and elevator. Suddenly she had this magical, wonderful power; whoever laid eyes on her smiled. **And the English language dwindled to a single word**, repeated over and over: "Congratulations!"

We walked—we floated—around the block to burn off our excess energy. Back at the hotel we were invited into the nightclub, even though Susan and I were underage. We drank ginger ales and ordered jalapeño poppers and we all danced to a country and western band while Susan's face beamed on the late news from the TV above the bar. The dance floor was the only

....

washed her in lights turned their lights on her

And the English language dwindled to a single word And there was only one word that everyone said place where she did not carry her silver plate.

First thing next morning there she was, sliding under the door of my hotel room: her picture on the front page of the *Arizona Republic*. I sat on the edge of the bed and stared at it, **pride welling in me**. I read the story. It called her speech **"mesmerizing, hypnotic, mysteriously touching."** I pictured folded morning papers tossed from cars, landing in driveways all over Mica.

We all met for the breakfast buffet. People stared and nodded and smiled and silently lip-said "Congratulations" across the restaurant. We headed for home in a two-car caravan.

For a while, Susan was her usual chatty self. She put the silver plate on the front seat beside Mr. McShane. She told him it would ride next to him for ten whole minutes, and he could touch it all he wanted. This was his reward, she said, for telling her about moas. As soon as the ten minutes was up, she took back the plate.

As we drew nearer to town, the chatter subsided and finally stopped. We rode the last miles in silence. She took my hand. The nearer we came the harder she squeezed. When we **hit the outskirts** of town, she turned to me and said, "Do I look okay?"

I told her she looked great.

She didn't seem to believe me. She held up the silver plate and studied her reflection.

She turned to me again and looked at me for some time

....

pride welling in me feeling very proud

"mesmerizing, hypnotic, mysteriously touching"
"interesting, special, personal"

hit the outskirts got to the edge

before she spoke. "I've been thinking. This is how I'm going to do it. I'm going to hold on to the plate myself—okay?"

I nodded.

" . . . until . . . until they lift me onto their shoulders. Then I give it to you. Understand?"

I nodded.

"So stay next to me. Every second. Crowds can separate you, you know. They do that. Okay?"

I nodded. "Okay."

Her hand was hot and sweating.

We drove past a man in his driveway. He was dipping a large, broomlike brush into a pail and painting the asphalt with black sealer. He was bent intently to his work in the noonday sun, and somehow I knew at that moment what would happen, I could see it. I wanted to shout to Mr. McShane, "No, don't turn! Don't go there!"

But he did turn. He turned, and there was the school in front of us, and never in my life have I seen a place so empty. No banners, no people, no cars.

"Probably around back," Mr. McShane said. His voice was **hoarse**. "Parking lot."

We **swung** around back to the parking lot and—yes—there was a car, and another car. And people, three of them, shading their eyes in the sun, watching us. Two of them were teachers. The other was a student, Dori Dilson. She stood apart from the teachers, alone in the black shimmering sea of asphalt. As we approached, she held up a sign, a huge cardboard sign bigger

....

hoarse rough
swung drove

than a basketball backboard. She set the sign on edge and propped it up, **erasing** herself. The red painted letters said:

WAY TO GO,
SUSAN
WE'RE PROUD OF
YOU

The car stopped in front of it. All that was left to see of Dori Dilson were two sets of fingers holding the sides of the sign. We were close enough now to see that the sign was trembling, and I knew that behind it Dori was crying. There was no confetti, no kazoos. Nothing cheered, not even a mockingbird.

....

erasing hiding

BEFORE YOU MOVE ON...

1. **Inference** Susan thinks it is important to be popular. Why? Reread pages 158–159.

2. **Mood** How does the mood of the story change when Susan returns from the contest?

LOOK AHEAD Read pages 175–189 to see how Susan reacts to the empty lot.

30

As we idled, stunned and silent in front of Dori Dilson's sign, Susan's parents came and retrieved her from Mr. McShane's car. As in all things, they did not appear especially surprised or emotional over what was happening. Susan seemed **in a trance**. She sat beside me, staring **vacantly** at the sign through the windshield. Her hand was no longer holding mine. **I groped for words but could not find them.** When her parents came, she allowed herself to be led away. As she got out of the car, the silver plate slid from her lap and rang like a dying bell against the asphalt. Her father picked it up. I thought he would take it, but instead he leaned into the back seat where I sat and with a strange smile gave it to me.

I did not see her for the rest of the weekend. By Monday she was Stargirl again. Floor-length skirt. Ribbons in her hair. Just like that.

She went from table to table at lunchtime, passing out happy-face cookies. She even gave one to Hillari Kimble. Hillari took off her shoe and used it like a hammer to smash the cookie on her table. Stargirl strolled among us strumming her ukulele, asking for requests. Cinnamon perched on her shoulder. He was strapped onto a tiny toy ukulele. She made her voice squeaky and kept her lips from moving and it was as if Cinnamon were serenading with her. Dori Dilson, bless her, stood and applauded. She was the only one. I was too stunned to

....

in a trance like she was in a dream

vacantly with no expression

I groped for words but could not find them. I could not think of anything to say.

join her. And too cowardly. And angry. And not wanting to show approval for her return to Stargirl. Most of the students did not even look, did not even seem to listen. At the bell, as we left the lunchroom, I looked back. The tables were littered with cookies.

Walking with her after school that day, I said, "I guess you're giving up, huh?"

She looked at me. "Giving up? On what?"

"On being popular. On being . . . " How could I say it?

She smiled. "Normal?"

I shrugged.

"Yes," she said firmly.

"Yes?"

"I'm answering your question. The answer is yes. I'm giving up on trying to be popular and normal." Her face and **body language** did not seem to match her words. She looked cheery, perky. So did Cinnamon, perched on her shoulder.

"Don't you think maybe you should back off a little?" I said. **"Don't come on so strong?"**

She smiled at me. She reached out and brushed the tip of my nose with her fingertip. "Because we live in a world of *them*, right? You told me that once."

We stared at each other. She kissed me on the cheek and walked away. She turned and said, "I know you're not going to ask me to the Ocotillo Ball. It's okay." She gave me her smile of infinite kindness and understanding, the smile I had seen her aim at so many other **needy souls**, and in that moment I hated her.

....

body language the way her body moved

"Don't come on so strong?" "You should try not to be so different."

needy souls sad people

That very night, as if he were playing a scripted role, Kevin called me and said, "So, who are you taking to the Ocotillo Ball?"

I dodged. "Who are *you* taking?"

"Don't know," he said.

"I don't either."

There was a pause on the other end of the line. "Not Stargirl?"

"Not necessarily," I said.

"You trying to tell me something?"

"What would I want to tell you?"

"I thought you were a **two**. I thought there was no question."

"So why are you asking?" I said, and hung up.

In bed that night, I became more and more uncomfortable as the moonlight crept up my sheet. I did something I had never done before. I pulled down the shade. In my dreams the old man on the mall bench raised a wobbling head and croaked, "How dare you forgive me."

Next morning there was a new item on the plywood roadrunner, a sheet of white paper. At the top it said:

Sign Up Here to Join
New Musical Group,
THE UKEE DOOKS
No Experience Necessary

....

I dodged. I avoided the question.

two couple

There were two numbered columns for names, forty in all. By the end of the day all forty were filled in, with names such as Minnie Mouse and Darth Vader and The Swamp Thing. The principal's name was there, too. And Wayne Parr. And Dori Dilson.

"Did you see?" said Kevin. "Somebody wrote in Parr's name."

We were in the studio control room. It was May and our *Hot Seats* were over for the year, but on some days we still **gravitated** to the studio after school.

"I saw," I said.

He stepped up to a blank monitor, studied his reflection. "So, I didn't see your name on the list."

"Nope."

"You don't want to be a Ukee Dook?"

"Guess not."

We **fiddled** with the equipment for a while. Kevin walked out onto the stage. He flipped a switch. His mouth moved, but I couldn't hear. I held the soft pad of a headphone against my ear. His voice seemed to come from another world. "She's turning goofy again, isn't she? Worse than ever."

I stared at him through the glass. I put down the headphone and walked out.

I understood what he was doing. He had decided that it was now okay to say bad things about Stargirl. **Permission to do so must have come from my behavior.** Apparently the first to read me was Stargirl herself. I still felt the sting from her

....

gravitated went

fiddled played

Permission to do so must have come from my behavior. He insulted her because I acted like I did not care.

178

remark about the Ocotillo Ball.

Was I that obvious?

Classrooms, hallways, courtyard, lunchroom—everywhere I went I heard her disparaged, mocked, slurred. Her attempt to become popular, to be more like them, had been a total failure. If anything, they detested her more now. And they were **more vocal** about it around me. Or was I just listening better?

She and Dori Dilson, the only Ukee Dooks, did a duet in the courtyard one day after school. Stargirl strummed the ukulele and they both sang "Blue Hawaii." Clearly, they had been practicing. They were very good. They were also very ignored. By the end of the song, they were the only two left in the courtyard.

Next day they were there again. This time they wore sombreros. They sang Mexican songs. "Cielito Lindo." "Vaya Con Dios, My Darling." I stayed inside the school. I was afraid to walk on past them, as if they weren't there. I was equally afraid to stand and listen. I peeked from a window. Stargirl was **doing her best imitation of a flamenco**; the click of **castanets** came through the windowpane.

Students walked past, most of them not even glancing her way. I saw Wayne Parr and Hillari Kimble go past, Hillari laughing out loud. And Kevin. And the basketball guys. I realized now that the shunning would never end. And I knew what I should do. I should go out there and stand in front of them and applaud. I should show Stargirl and the world that

....

more vocal talking louder
doing her best imitation of a flamenco trying to dance
castanets Spanish percussion instruments

I wasn't like the rest of them, that I appreciated her, that I celebrated her and her **insistence on being** herself. But I stayed inside. I waited until the last of the students had left the courtyard, and Stargirl and Dori were performing for no one. To my surprise they went on and on. It was too painful to watch. I left school by another door.

....

insistence on being determination to be

31

As she had predicted, I did not ask her to the Ocotillo Ball. I did not ask anyone. I did not go.

She did.

The ball took place on a Saturday night in late May on the tennis courts of the Mica Country Club. When sunset was **down to a faintly glowing ember** in the west and the moon rose in the east, I went forth on my bicycle. I coasted by the club. **Festooned with Cantonese** lanterns, the ball in the distance looked like a cruise ship at sea.

I could not identify individuals, only **stirrings** of color. Much of it was powder blue. The day after Wayne Parr said he had chosen powder blue for his dinner jacket, three-quarters of the boys ordered the same from Tuxedo Junction.

Back and forth I **cruised** in the night beyond the lights. Music reached my ears as random peeps. The desert flowers, so abundant in April, were dying now. I had the notion that they were calling to each other.

I cruised for hours. The moon rose into the sky like a lost balloon. Somewhere in the dark shapes of the Maricopas, a coyote howled.

In the days and weeks and years that followed, everyone agreed: they had never seen anything like it.

She arrived in a bicycle sidecar. Just big enough for her to sit in, the sidecar had a single outboard wheel. The inboard side

....

down to a faintly glowing ember almost over
Festooned with Cantonese Decorated with Chinese
stirrings movements
cruised rode my bike

was braced to the bike. Everything but the seat of the bike and the sidecar bench was covered in flowers. A ten-foot blanket of flowers trailed the rear fender like a **bridal train**. Palm fronds flared from the handlebars. It looked like a float in the Rose Parade. Dori Dilson pedaled the bicycle.

Eyewitnesses later filled in what I could not see: parents' cameras flashing, floodlights making a second day as the gorgeous couples disembark from limos and borrowed convertibles and promenade to the festive courts. **Showers of applause.** Suddenly the flashing stops, the floodlights dim, a hush falls over the crowd. As a particularly long white limo rolls away from the entrance, here comes this three-wheeled bouquet.

The driver Dori Dilson wears a tailed white tuxedo and tall silk hat, but it is her passenger who rivets the crowd. Her strapless gown is a bright, rich yellow, as if pressed from buttercups. There must be one of those hooped contraptions underneath, for the skirt billows outward from her waist like an upside-down teacup. Her hair is incredible. **Descriptions clash.** Some say it is the color of honey, some say strawberries. It fluffs like a meringue high upon her head. It's a wig. No, it's all hers. Both sides are certain.

Earrings dangle. They are little silver somethings. But what? They are partly obscured by falling **ringlets**. Many answers are offered. The most popular is Monopoly pieces, but this will prove to be wrong.

From a rawhide string around her neck dangles a white

---

bridal train long wedding dress
Showers of applause. A lot of clapping.
Descriptions clash. Everyone describes her hair differently.
ringlets curls

inch-long banana-shaped fossil identifying her as a member in good standing of the Loyal Order of the Stone Bone.

While others wear orchids, the corsage on her wrist is a small sunflower. Or a huge black-eyed Susan. Or some sort of daisy. No one is sure, except that the colors are yellow and black.

Before proceeding, she turns back to the bicycle and bends over a small basket hanging from the handlebars. The basket, too, is covered with flowers. She appears to kiss something in it. She then waves to Dori Dilson, Dori salutes, and the bicycle pulls away. People nearby catch a glimpse of tiny cinnamon-colored ears and two peppercorn eyes peering out of the basket.

"Beautiful."

"Unusual."

"Interesting."

"Different."

"Regal."

These words will come later from the parents **lining the walk**. For now, there are only stares as she makes her way from the entrance to the ball. Someone recalls a single camera flashing, but that is all. **She is no one's child.** She is the girl they have heard about. As she passes by she makes no attempt to avoid their eyes. On the contrary, she looks directly at them, turning to one side, then the other, looking into their eyes and smiling as if she knows them, as if they have shared grand and special things. Some turn aside, uneasy in a way they cannot account for; others feel suddenly empty when her eyes leave

---

"Regal." "Royal."

lining the walk who were standing by the walkway

She is no one's child. No one knows her.

theirs. So distracting, so complete is she that she is gone before many realize that she had no escort, she was alone, a parade of one.

Perched on my bike in the distance, I remember looking up and seeing the **torrent** of stars we call the Milky Way. I remember wondering if she could see them, too, or were they lost in the light of the lanterns?

The dancing took place on the center tennis court, which had been covered with a portable parquet floor. She did what everyone else did at the ball: she danced. To the music of Guy Greco and the Serenaders she danced the slow dances and the fast ones. She spread her arms wide and threw back her head and closed her eyes and gave every impression of thoroughly enjoying herself. They did not speak to her, of course, but they could not help looking over the shoulders of their dates. She clapped at the end of each **number**.

She's alone, they kept telling themselves, and surely she danced in no one's arms, yet somehow that seemed to matter less and less. As the night went on, and clarinet and coyote call mingled beyond the lantern light, the magic of their own powder-blue jackets and orchids seemed to fade, and **it came to them in small sensations** that they were more alone than she was.

Who was the first to crack? No one knows. Did someone brush against her at the punch table? Pluck a petal from her flower? (One was missing.) Whisper "Hi"? This much is

....

torrent large group

number song

it came to them in small sensations the students started to realize certain: a boy named Raymond Studemacher danced with her.

To the student body at large, Raymond Studemacher **did not have enough substance to trigger the opening of a supermarket door**. He belonged to no team or organization. He took part in no school activities. His grades were ordinary. His clothing was ordinary. His face was ordinary. He had no detectable personality. Thin as a minute, he appeared to lack the heft to carry his own name. And in fact, when all eyes turned to him on the dance floor, those few who came up with a name for him frowned at his white jacket and whispered, "Raymond Something."

And yet there he was, Raymond Something, walking right up to her—it came out later that his date had suggested it—and speaking to her, and then they were dancing. Couples steered themselves to get a better look. At the end of the number, he joined her in clapping and returned to his date. He told her the silver earrings looked like little trucks.

Tension rose. Boys got antsy. Girls picked at their corsages. **The ice shattered.** Several boys broke from their dates. They were heading her way when she walked up to Guy Greco and said something to him. Guy Greco turned to the Serenaders, the baton flashed, and out came the sounds of that old teen dance standard: the bunny hop. Within seconds a long line was snaking across the dance floor. Stargirl led the way. And suddenly it was December again, and **she had the school in her spell**.

Almost every couple joined in. Hillari Kimble and Wayne

....

did not have enough substance to trigger the opening of a supermarket door was not special

The ice shattered. The mood changed.

she had the school in her spell everyone liked her

Parr did not.

The line curled back and forth across the netless tennis courts. Stargirl began to **improvise**. She flung her arms to a make-believe crowd like a celebrity on parade. She waggled her fingers at the stars. She churned her fists like an eggbeater. Every action echoed down the line behind her. The three hops of the bunny became three struts of a vaudeville vamp. Then a penguin waddle. Then a tippy-toed priss. Every new move brought new laughter from the line.

When Guy Greco ended the music, howls of protest greeted him. **He restruck the downbeat.**

To delighted squeals, Stargirl led them off the parquet dance floor onto the other courts—and then through the chain-link fence and off the tennis courts altogether. Red carnations and wrist corsages flashed as the line headed onto the practice putting green of the golf course. The line doodled around the holes, in and out of sidepools of lantern light. From the dance floor it seemed to be more than it was: one hundred couples, two hundred people, four hundred dancing legs seemed to be a single festive flowery creature, a fabulous millipede. And then there was less and less to see as the head vanished and the rest curled through the fringe of the light and followed, like the tail of a powder-blue dragon, into the darkness.

One girl in chiffon had a **tiff** with her date and ran off toward the first tee, calling, "Wait for me!" She looked like a huge mint-green moth.

Their voices came in clearly from the golf course. The

....

improvise create new dance moves

He restruck the downbeat. He kept playing the music.

tiff fight

laughing and yelping **made a raucous counterpoint to the metronomic** *tock-tock-tock* of the bunny's never-ending hop. Once, in the light of the quarter moon, they appeared in silhouette on a domed, distant green, like figures dancing in someone's dream.

And then quite suddenly they were gone, as if the dreamer had awakened. Nothing to see, nothing to hear. Someone called "Hey!" after them, but that was all.

It was, according to those left behind, like waiting for a diver in water to return to the surface. Hillari Kimble, for one, did not share that feeling. "I came here to dance," she declared. She pulled Wayne Parr along to the bandstand and demanded "regular music."

Guy Greco tilted his head to listen, but the baton did not stop and neither did the band.

In fact, as the minutes went by, the music seemed to become louder. Maybe it was **an illusion**. Maybe the band felt a connection to the dancers. Maybe the farther the line spun into the night, the louder the band had to play. Maybe the music was a **tether**. Or a kite string.

Hillari Kimble dragged Wayne Parr out to the middle of the parquet floor. They slowdanced. They fastdanced. They even tried an old-fashioned jitterbug. Nothing worked. Nothing went with the triple-thumping drumbeat but the bunny hop itself. Hillari's orchid shed petals as she beat her fist on Wayne Parr's chest. "Do something!" she yelled. She ripped sticks of chewing gum from his pocket. She chewed them furiously.

··

made a raucous counterpoint to the metronomic was in the same rhythm of the

an illusion not really happening

tether rope

She split the wad and pressed the gum into her ears.

The band played on.

Afterward, there were many different guesses as to how long the bunny-hoppers were actually gone. Everyone agreed it seemed to be hours. Students stood under the last line of lanterns, their fingers curling through the plastic-coated wire of the fence, peering into the vast blackness, straining for a glimpse, a scrap of sound. All they heard was the call of a coyote. A boy dashed wildly into the darkness; he **sauntered** back, his blue jacket over his shoulder, laughing. A girl with glitter in her hair shivered. Her bare shoulders shook as if she were cold. She began to cry.

Hillari Kimble **stalked** along the fence, clenching and unclenching her fists. She could not seem to stand still.

When the call finally came—"They're back!"—it was from a lone watcher at the far end. A hundred kids—only Hillari Kimble stayed behind—turned and raced down eight tennis courts, pastel skirts flapping like stampeding flamingos. The fence buckled outward as they slammed into it. They strained to see. Light barely trickled over crusted earth beyond the fence. This was the desert side.

"Where? . . . Where?"

And then you could hear: whoops and yahoos out there, somewhere, clashing with the music. And then—*there!*—a flash of yellow, Stargirl leaping from the shadows. The rest followed out of the darkness, a long, powder-blue, **many-headed birthing**. *Hop-hop-hop.* They were still **smack on the beat.**

....

sauntered walked slowly
stalked walked angrily
many-headed birthing group of people appearing
smack on the beat dancing perfectly to the music

If anything, they seemed more energized than before. They were fresh. Their eyes sparkled in the lantern light. Many of the girls wore browning, half-dead flowers in their hair.

Stargirl led them along the outside of the fence. Those inside got up a line of their own and hopped along. Guy Greco struck the downbeat three final times—*hop-hop-hop*—and the two lines **collided** at the gate in a frenzy of hugs and shrieks and kisses.

Shortly after, as the Serenaders gratefully played "Stardust," Hillari Kimble walked up to Stargirl and said, "You ruin everything." And she slapped her.

The crowd grew instantly still. The two girls stood facing each other for a long minute. Those nearby saw in Hillari's shoulders and eyes **a flinching**: she was waiting to be struck in reply. And in fact, when Stargirl finally moved, Hillari winced and shut her eyes. But it was lips that touched her, not the palm of a hand. Stargirl kissed her gently on the cheek. She was gone by the time Hillari opened her eyes.

Dori Dilson was waiting. Stargirl seemed to float down the promenade in her buttercup gown. She climbed into the sidecar, the flowered bicycle rolled off into the night, and that was the **last any of us ever saw of her**.

....

collided met each other

a flinching some movement

last any of us ever saw of her last time we ever saw her

BEFORE YOU MOVE ON...

1. **Character's Motive** Why does Susan go back to being Stargirl?

2. **Conclusions** Reread pages 177–179. Leo knows he is being a bad person. How can you tell?

LOOK AHEAD Read to page 200 to see what Leo discovers about Stargirl.

32

That was fifteen years ago. Fifteen Valentine's Days.

I remember that sad summer after the Ocotillo Ball just as clearly as everything else. One day, feeling needy, empty, I walked over to her house. A For Sale sign **pierced** the ground out front. I peered through a window. Nothing but bare walls and floors.

I went to see Archie. Something in his smile said he had been expecting me. We sat on the back porch. Everything seemed as usual. Archie lighting his pipe. The desert golden in the evening sun. Señor Saguaro losing his pants.

Nothing had changed.

Everything had changed.

"Where?" I said.

A corner of his mouth winked open and a silky rumple of smoke emerged, paused as if to be admired, then drifted off past his ear. "Midwest. Minnesota."

"Will I ever see her again?"

He shrugged. "Big country. Small world. Who knows?"

"She didn't even finish out the school year."

"Just . . . **vamoosed**."

"Mm-hm."

"It's only been weeks, but it seems like a dream. Was she really here? Who was she? Was she real?"

He looked at me for a long time, his smile wry, his eyes

------

pierced stood firmly in
vamoosed disappeared

twinkling. Then he shook his head as if coming out of a trance. He **deadpanned**, "Oh, you're waiting for an answer. What were the questions again?"

"Stop being **nutty**, Archie."

He looked off to the west. The sun was **melting butter over the Maricopas**. "Real? Oh, yes. As real as we get. Don't ever doubt that. That's the good news." He pointed the pipe stem at me. "And well named. Stargirl. Though I think she had simpler things in mind. Star people are rare. You'll be lucky to meet another."

"Star people?" I said. "You're losing me here."

He chuckled. "That's okay. I lose myself. It's just my oddball way of accounting for someone I don't really understand any more than you do."

"So where do stars come in?"

He pointed the pipe stem. "The perfect question. In the beginning, that's where they come in. They supplied the ingredients that became us, the primordial elements. We are star stuff, yes?" He held up the skull of Barney, the Paleocene rodent. "Barney, too, hm?"

I nodded, along for the ride.

"And I think every once in a while someone comes along who is a little more **primitive** than the rest of us, a little closer to our beginnings, a little more in touch with the stuff we're made of."

The words seemed to fit her, though I could not grasp their meaning.

....

deadpanned joked
nutty silly
melting butter over the Maricopas setting
primitive natural

He saw the vacant look on my face and laughed. He tossed Barney to me. He stared at me. "She liked you, boy."

The intensity of his voice and eyes made me blink.

"Yes," I said.

"She did it for you, you know."

"What?"

"**Gave up her self**, for a while there. She loved you that much. What an incredibly lucky kid you were."

I could not look at him. "I know."

He shook his head with a **wistful** sadness. "No, you don't. You can't know yet. Maybe someday . . . "

I knew he was tempted to say more. Probably to tell me how stupid I was, how cowardly, that I **blew** the best chance I would ever have. But his smile returned, and his eyes were tender again, and nothing harsher than cherry smoke came out of his mouth.

I continued to attend Saturday meetings of the Loyal Order of the Stone Bone. We did not speak of her again until the following summer, several days before I was to leave for college. Archie had asked me to come over.

He took me out back, but this time not to the porch. Instead he led me to the toolshed. He slid back the bolt and opened the door and—it was not a toolshed after all. "This was her office," he said and gestured for me to enter.

Here it was: all the stuff of her activity that I had expected to see in her room at home, the "office" whose location she

....

Gave up her self Stopped being who she really was
wistful thoughtful
blew ruined

would not reveal. I saw wheels of ribbon and wrapping paper, stacks of colored construction paper, cardboard boxes of newspaper clippings, watercolors and cans of paint, a yellow stack of phone books.

Tacked to one wall was a municipal map of Mica. Hundreds of pins of a dozen different colors pierced the map. **There was no indication what they stood for.** A huge homemade calendar covered the opposite wall. It had a square for every date in the year. Penciled into the squares were names. Across the top of the calendar was one word: BIRTHDAYS. There was one dot of color on the whole thing, a little red heart. It was next to my name.

Archie handed me a fat family album sort of book. The homemade title said "The Early Life of Peter Sinkowitz." I flipped through it. I saw the pictures she had taken that day: Peter squabbling with the little girls over his beloved banana roadster.

"I'm to wait five years, then give it to his parents," said Archie.

He pointed to a filing cabinet in the corner.

It had three drawers. I opened one. There were dozens of red hanging folders, each with a name tag sticking up. I saw "Borlock." Me. I pulled it out, opened it. There was the birthday notice that appeared in the Mica Times three years before. And a **profile of me** from the school paper. And pictures: **candid snapshots** of me in a parking lot, me leaving my house, me at the mall. Apparently, Peter Sinkowitz wasn't

....

There was no indication what they stood for. I could not tell why they were there.

profile of me short article about me

candid snapshots random photographs

the only target for her camera. And a sheet of paper with two columns: "Likes" and "Doesn't Like." Heading the list of "Likes" was "porcupine neckties." Under that was "strawberry-banana smoothies."

I replaced my folder. I saw other names. Kevin. Dori Dilson. Mr. McShane. Danny Pike. Anna Grisdale. Even Hillari Kimble and Wayne Parr.

I stepped back. I was stunned.

"This is . . . unbelievable. Files. On people. Like she was a spy."

Archie nodded, smiling. "A **lovely treason**, hm?"

I could not speak. He led me out into the dazzling light.

....

lovely treason nice secret

33

Throughout my college years I visited Archie whenever I came home. And then I got a job back East, and my visits were less frequent. As Archie grew older, the difference between himself and Señor Saguaro seemed to become less and less. We sat on the back porch. He seemed fascinated by my work. I had become a **set designer**. Only recently has it occurred to me that I became one on the day Stargirl took me to her enchanted place.

On my last visit with him, he met me at the front door. He dangled keys in front of my eyes. "You drive."

An old tar pail rattled in the bed of his ancient pickup as he pointed me west to the Maricopas. In his lap he carried a brown paper bag.

Along the way I said, as I always did, "So, have you figured her out yet?"

It was years since she had gone, yet still we needed no name for her. We knew who we were talking about.

"I'm working on it," he said.

"What's the latest?"

We were following a familiar script.

On this day he stated: "She's better than bones." On my previous visit, he had said, "When a Stargirl cries, she does not shed tears, but light." On other days in other years, he had called her "the rabbit in the hat" and "the universal solvent" and

....

set designer person who builds sets for plays or movies
We were following a familiar script. We were saying things
we had said before.

"the recycler of our garbage."

He said these things with a sly grin, knowing they would
confound me as I mulled them until our next meeting.

We were in the foothills by early afternoon. He directed me
to stop on a stony shoulder of the road. We got out and walked.
He brought the paper bag with him. I brought the pail. He
pulled from it a floppy blue hat, which he mashed onto his head.
The sun that had looked warm and buttery at a distance was
blazing hot here.

We didn't go far, as walking was a chore for him. We
stopped at an outcropping of smooth, pale-gray rock. He pulled
a small pick from the pail and tapped the rock. "This'll do," he
said.

I held the paper bag while he **put pick to rock**. The skin
on his arms had become dry and flaky, as if his body were
preparing itself to rejoin the earth. It took him ten minutes to
gouge out a hole that he judged to be right.

He asked for the bag. I was shocked at what he took from it.

"Barney!"

The skull of the Paleocene rodent.

"This is home," he said. He said he was sorry he did not
have the energy to return Barney to his original **stratum** in
South Dakota. He laid Barney in the hole, then took from his
pocket a scrap of paper. He crumpled the scrap and stuffed it
into the hole with the skull. Then he pulled a jug of water, a
small bag of patching cement, a **trowel**, and a plastic tray from

----

confound confuse
put pick to rock dug a hole
stratum layer of earth or rock
trowel shovel

the tar pail. He mixed the cement and **troweled over** the hole. From a distance you wouldn't know the rock had been **altered**.

Heading back to the pickup, I asked him what was written on the paper.

"A word," he said. The way he said it told me I'd get no answer to the next question.

We rode east down out of the mountains and were home before sundown.

When I returned next time, someone else was living in Archie's house. The shed out back was gone. So was Señor Saguaro.

And a new elementary school now occupies Stargirl's enchanted place.

....

troweled over covered
altered changed

MORE THAN STARS

Since graduating, our class has had a reunion every five years, but I haven't yet gone. I stay in touch with Kevin. He never left Mica, has a family there now. Like me, he did not **wind up** in television, but he does make good use of his **gift of gab**: he's an insurance salesman.

Kevin says when the class gathers for reunions at the Mica Country Club, there is much talk of Stargirl and curiosity **as to her whereabouts**. He says the most common question these days is "Were you on the bunny hop?" At the last reunion several classmates, for a lark, lined up, hands to waists, and hopped around the putting green for a few minutes, but it wasn't the same.

No one is quite sure what happened to Wayne Parr, except that he and Hillari broke up shortly after graduation. The last anyone heard, he spoke of joining the Coast Guard.

The high school has a new club called the Sunflowers. To

....

wind up get a career
gift of gab love of talking
as to her whereabouts about where she is

join, you have to sign an agreement promising to do "one nice thing per day for someone other than myself."

Today's Electron marching band is probably the only one in Arizona with a ukulele.

On the basketball court, the Electrons have never come close to the success they enjoyed when I was a junior. But something from that season has **resurfaced** in recent years that baffles fans from other schools. At every game, when the opposing team scores its first basket, a small group of Electrons fans jumps to its feet and cheers.

Each time I visit Mica, I drive past her old house on Palo Verde. On the most recent visit, I saw a red-haired young man across the street, fixing water skis to the roof of a yellow Volkswagen Beetle. It must have been Peter Sinkowitz. I wondered if he was as possessive of his Beetle as he had been of the banana roadster. I wondered if he was old enough to love his scrapbook.

As for me, I **throw myself into my work and keep an eye peeled** for silver lunch trucks, and I remember. I sometimes walk in the rain without an umbrella. When I see change on the sidewalk, I leave it there. If no one's looking, I drop a quarter. I feet guilty when I buy a card from Hallmark. I listen for mockingbirds.

I read the newspapers. I read them from all over. I skip the front pages and headlines and go to the pages in back. I read the community sections and the fillers. I see little acts of kindness happening from Maine to California. I read of a man

....

resurfaced started to happen again
throw myself into my work and keep an eye peeled work very hard and watch

in Kansas City who stands at a busy intersection every morning and waves at the people driving to work. I read of a little girl in Oregon who sells lemonade in front of her house for five cents a cup—and offers a free back scratch to every customer.

When I read about things like these I wonder, *Is she there?* I wonder what she calls herself now. I wonder if she's lost her freckles. I wonder if I'll ever get another chance. I wonder, but I don't **despair**. Though I have no family of my own, I do not feel alone. I know that I am being watched. **The echo of her laughter is the second sunrise I awaken to each day**, and at night I feel it is more than stars looking down on me. Last month, one day before my birthday, I received a gift-wrapped package in the mail. It was a porcupine necktie.

....

despair lose hope

The echo of her laughter is the second sunrise I awaken to each day I remember the sound of her laughter each day and it makes me happy

BEFORE YOU MOVE ON...

1. **Conclusions** Why is Leo telling Stargirl's story even though it has been fifteen years?

2. **Inference** Stargirl is still thinking about Leo. How do you know this?

200